into AFRICA

into AFRICA

An exciting sequel to Stepfather's Manipulation

TOM WEST

authorHOUSE®

AuthorHouse™ UK
1663 Liberty Drive
Bloomington, IN 47403 USA
www.authorhouse.co.uk
Phone: 0800.197.4150

Published by AuthorHouse 05/15/2015

ISBN: 978-1-5049-4297-3 (sc)
ISBN: 978-1-5049-4296-6 (e)

Print information available on the last page.

The announcement came over the tannoy.

"This is your captain speaking."

"Food and beverages will be served shortly,"

This announcement prepared the airhostesses, ordered by the captain.

The lights came on: passengers started to roll up their window blinds. As the Sun beamed into the cabin. Tables down and suddenly two more gorgeous airhostesses appeared with food, fit for a King and Queen. My sisters, Princesses and I the Prince, really. Well, suppose we like to think of our family of Princess's. As we certainly felt like royalty sitting on those big comfortable chairs. Being waited on hand and foot, served with the finest food and drinks that one could ever ask for, one family could expect on this fabulous aircraft.

Hello and welcome to the second book.

Into Africa

The noise from the plane was buzzing my ears. A soft background noise was rumbling from the engines as we are flying at 30,000 feet on a subsonic route to Africa. It is dazzling in the aircraft cabin. As the sun has come up with a beautiful sunrise, on a bright, crisp, beautiful morning everybody around sitting in chairs resting doing their own little thing, in their thoughts. What can one believe just by picking out a person and reading their mind, I thought to pass the time. Now how would I do that? Is it not, just a reflection of their personality painting the visual picture through their body language and facial expressions is this, really possible to read? An expression on someone's face, an expression of happiness or sadness, can this determine what is going on inside his or her mind. Many different looks many different emotions many different thoughts within the mind. All these thoughts at 30,000 feet. Looking at Amanda she's fast asleep with her headphones in her ears, no doubt there is music or a film playing on her headphones. She seems to be so contented and comfortable. In addition, Denise is in a state of pure relaxation while she is watching the end of a film, (also wearing headphones.) Myself, I am sitting in the middle not at either end, just in the midst of the three seats, and two sisters, not even a window seat or not even the aisle seat. I felt entirely closed in but very comfortable as I could be. As I reclined my chair, looking straight up at the console above my head. I could see the Air Conditioning nozzles, lights for the individual seats, airhostess button. Suddenly my sister Denise sits up in her chair and pushes the airhostess button, for assistance. This button lights up immediately with an orange glow, as my sister sits down a few moments later; an airhostess turns up. How may I help you miss after the airhostess reached across and pressed the button once more to stop the Orange Flashing Glow? Denise says, "thank you for coming how long are we away from landing." Denise asks. After breakfast, the airhostess says. It will not be long now. As we are just serving, miss. Is there anything else that I can get you? Denise says. May I have a drink, please? "Oh yes." "Miss what would you like?" "A can of Coke please, immediately drawing to Tom's attention; politely asking the hostess, "may I also have a can of Coke for myself." "Please," the airhostess asks my sister, and I "am that all Miss, Sir, Yes thank you. Denise and I said. As the airhostess walked away down the aisle, we noticed the hostess trolley was just coming through the curtains. The sunlight is shining brightly across the hostess trolley. Under a minute later, the air stewardess came back with our drinks on a silver tray, with two glasses filled with ice. "What a perfect morning Denise says looking through the window." Pulling down her table at the same time as Tom. As the airhostess placed the glasses on the table. Denise was 1st.

Then mine with a smile. Pouring the refreshing drink over the ice cubes. Making! A lovely Refreshing chinking sound in the glass. For this is into apparently so relaxing. I was watching the ice swirl around in the glass as the Coca-Cola flooded the ice cubes; the Bubbles were breaking the surface of my fizzy drink, pouring down in mid-air just like miniature fireworks. With this Fizzing fresh sound, as the crystal glass filled. I am sure that I will now never forget. Along with everything else the beautiful air hostesses on this flight. You can well imagine the excitement of our first trip, seeing the first breathtaking beautiful clear, bright sunrise at 30,000 feet. In the heavens. My sister was amazed at the view from the window. How big! The world seems, Denise, said. "I have never seen it like this before." "Only ever seen it in books," but it has never looked so beautiful as I could not imagine how breathtaking it could be." "Which you cannot beat the real thing," I said. Denise totally agreed with me. Acknowledging Tom, with a smile. Moreover, we both gazed out of the window taking in the breathtaking scenery landscapes and clouds, taking a moment or two to have a sip of our tasty, refreshing cool-Coke drinks. With bubbles tickling my nose. It did not take long for the hostess trolley to appear, the ladies, beautiful air hostesses politely asked all of us what would we like as Amanda started to wake. She must have been so tired of all the turmoil and the hard work, and responsibility that has undertaken at the airport. Alternatively, maybe it was something to do with all the complimentary mini drinks that she had the night before.

"Good morning, ladies and gentlemen Beverley said." "Hello," Beverley altogether as if in harmony with the lovely smile. Beverley beamed with a beautiful bright smile, in reply. Then started serving the breakfasts. This process was corrected so quickly and so professionally in excellent fluid way. To airhostesses one each side of the trolley serving each side of the aisle at the same time. It seemed like they were racing the other trolley on the other aisle. Nevertheless, it was in a competitive manner but never let go or losing their professional image to the customers. In addition, always service with a smile. As the air, hostesses may be serving approximately 400+ passengers if the plane is to capacity. In first, second and business class, so I must take this opportunity to say a big thank you to all airhostesses, you are doing a fantastic job many thanks. We appreciate you.

While Amanda is stretching yawning after her long Sleep. I reached across and lowered her table for Amanda as the lovely air hostess placed our breakfasts on the table one by one, while Amanda was rubbing her eyes trying to take the moment and realize that she is on the plane. I am sure you all know how this feels.

Waking up in a strange place, (unfamiliar surroundings slightly disorientated. For a moment!) Nevertheless, it only takes a few short minutes and Amanda is awake, saying good morning. Still with a little yawn on her mouth. What perfect timing to wake up for breakfast. I thought to myself.

Denise gently places a white cloth napkin on my lap. I also did the same for Amanda. The air hostesses appeared and disappeared as quick as they arrived. Serving the next customer in the perfect hostess manner treating everybody with professionalism and courteous combined with silver service and beauty. What a beautiful morning, this is turning out to be. I was thinking while I was peeling off the keep fresh tops from the in-flight continental breakfasts. The aroma of the hot food was just divine.

That made Toms tummy rumble. Moments later Tom and his sisters were gently unwrapping the cutlery out of cotton napkins. Saying grace so close to heaven felt unusual but dangerous. Getting started on our breakfast.

Amanda and Denise were both enjoying their meals also. Incredibly Delicious. Sausage, Bacon, Egg beans Mushrooms, cereals, and fresh orange juice, croissant all shared between us. A few moments later, another trolley appears with another beautiful air hostess serving tea, coffee, and cold drinks if we need. A cup of tea please Denise said and Amanda.

Tom was happy with a top up on my Coca-Cola. Which the air hostess served us in an elegant way. Moreover, then moved on to the next customers sitting down the aisles behind us. All I can say is it was just an incredible breakfast. I could not wish to be anywhere else but with my two sisters sitting on this magnificent plane enjoying fabulous food and fantastic company flying to new adventures within a tropical nation. Instantly I can see this is, what living is all surrounding? Here is what you get if you do everything correctly. Suddenly unexpectedly, we could hear a baby crying approximately two rows behind us. It must be the air pressure in the cabin. Under one-year-old baby did not know how to explain his ears; I thought to myself, it might be quite difficult for children to be in the airplane at such a young age. I could hear an air hostess assisting the mother with her young baby. Making sure that the mother and child, are as comfortable as possible. In addition, showing the mother how to clear the babies' ears. As this is the primary sources of discomfort for infants, Flying causes the changing atmospheric pressure in the inner ear, cabin pressure when taking off and landing. Aforementioned creates pressure in the ears and can be quite painful for your baby particularly if the baby has a stuffy nose. When flying with a baby, prepare for this by planning to nurse or give a bottle or pacifier to the child during takeoff and landing to help alleviate the pressure. Something is as simple as giving the baby a bottle to drink making him do that sucking action, and swallowing action helps the child clear their ears. I heard the mother saying thank you very much as the baby stops crying. I thought that the baby is happy now. In addition, a few minutes of professional care from the air hostess made mother and child another happy customer. Approximately, 20 to 25 min later air hostesses come round again with a trolley collecting all the empty breakfasts. Breakfast time is always a pleasant break from a long flight or journey in the plane.

Time to have a little wander around and a bathroom break I think. "Excuse me Denise," "where are you going" Denise Asked. "I am just going to have a wander around the cabin and a bathroom break" "would you like to come?" "I understand upstairs they have a lounge with a cocktail bar." "I had never seen one before," said Denise says that will be wonderful let's go and explore.

Brilliant I thought let us go and explore. Denise lets me out of my seat letting Amanda know where we are going just out of courteous.

Amanda knew where we were going as she overheard the conversation and did not want to come to visit the cocktail lounge on the upper deck. I understand, and it is within that small bump on top of the plane. Off we go. Walking down between long lines of seats. First remembering what is our seat number just to give us a little bit of a chance to get back. Denise and I were walking down the aisle through thick black curtains into a small corridor and then through another set of curtains into the first class. impressive. A little bit uneasy Denise felt, and I comforted her, just to give her more encouragement because I wanted to see this cocktail bar upstairs. That. I have heard people speaking about earlier. On my travels to the cockpit in the earlier volume. Just through another set of curtains and there was a spiral staircase leading upstairs. Quietly nervously, exploring, Denise and I walked up the first flight of stairs looking around at the same time taking in all the beauty and the fabulous architecture within the Jumbo jet airliner Denise and I have never seen such opulence. Then upon the second flight of stairs, now we are at the top of the massive Tri-Star Boeing 747 plane. Walking unwaveringly Straight with one thought in mind heading into the cocktail bar and lounge. The Stairs built out of shiny chrome steel, and steps happened carpeted the stairs were very broad just as if you would have in a large manor house. Very plush fabulous staircase.

Also, well lit.

The staircase spiral training in a big circle and then narrowed off as we got further up to the top flight of stairs.

On walking through the next curtain, we have a delightful experience to all of our senses when we see how well decorated and gorgeous the lounge was. Fitted shag pile carpets in cream leather sofas reclining chairs swivel chairs. The air hostesses were wearing different uniforms in the cocktail lounge bar.

Someone appeared from nowhere, could I help you, she said. Yes please, May we have a drink, please? Denise said that would be lovely thank you. The pleasing little smile on her face in fact we were both triumphal with the experience of just walking into this beautiful room. Feeling slightly nervous, but still nevertheless we were going to experience this magnificent place. You may take a seat the host mentioned. A very kind air hostess showed us to our seats. The smell of leather in the room was powerful along with their fantastic visual displays of beautiful marble, metal fixing high-quality values of the things that made a room pop with beauty. There was soft music playing in the background. Nice and relaxing. I think we can stay here for the rest of the trip. It is a shame Amanda is not here to share this experience with us. The lovely Airhostess arrived with our drinks again placing them down on a coaster. Enjoy your drinks, will that be all, the air hostess said.

Denise and I said with a smile, yes thank you. We spoke quietly among ourselves Denise and me, (as we were so excited.) Then unexpectedly somebody says, Hello Mr. West, how are you holding Sir. Very well thank You. A tall man in a black uniform with four gold stripes on his cuffs of his jacket and labels. It is the captain I recognized him immediately.

Captain Neil McCarthy, whom I was speaking to earlier in the cockpit. My sister Denise was overwhelmed. Still keeping her composure, I introduced my sister to the captain of the Tri-Star Boeing 747 airliner. Wow, what an experience. We feel like we are the number 1 people of the plane now in 1st class in the cocktail lounge talking to the captain of the Tri-Star Boeing 747, the flagship of British Airways. How much time do we have before we land in Africa? I asked we have approximately 2 hours before we start to descend Sir. Thank you captain.

Neil McCarthy, the captain, said, please enjoy the rest of your flight Denise looked straight into the captain's eyes and said it has been an enjoyable and pleasurable experience especially for our first flight ever. We have been very comfortable, thank you, and my brother Tom is over the moon for having the chance to visit the cockpit in this fabulous plane. The captain said. Very nice to hear that Miss thank you for your expression. Asking the question that, do you think that Tom would like to make a career as a pilot. I do not know Denise said, but Tom has not stopped telling us about his experience, he has enjoyed it so much.

Tom spoke out and said I would like to do this job. At that moment, another air hostess also appeared in a different uniform. Nodded to the captain the captain immediately responded and said, it is a pleasure meeting you both, please enjoy the rest of your journey, and I hope that you have a wonderful holiday in Africa. Please excuse me. He smiled and then stood up, turned around and walked away gracefully, but powerfully with authority walking through the door. Another air hostess in a burgundy uniform was holding that open for the captain.

Denise said I felt like we have just been speaking to royalty. I told you I was speechless with a smile. Both of us overwhelmed with the experience of sitting with the captain. It is a shame that we could not have had a photograph of all three of us, as this would have been pride of place in the photo album. Capturing a fond memory. We both agreed on this. However, we both carried on talking about a wonderful experience that we are going to see on this amazing holiday so far. We have not even got out of the plane yet. If this carries on this way. It is that we will not want to go back home. Denise said. I agree I whispered.

On the table, there was a pack of playing cards unopened in a box on the. I reach forward to pick up the pack of playing cards as the air hostess walked over she offered assistance to unwrap the playing cards as I was having difficulty opening the cellophane on the box. The skilled air hostess showed me the process of opening the pack of cards, by snapping them at first like a twig. Then sliding the deck of cards out-of-the-box like silk into her hand, asking me if I would like them ruffled. I nodded with a smile, then as if she was a professional casino croupier. She shuffled the cards with both hands. Making them into an ark at first the cards slid down together into a single pack once more, this air hostess repeated this several times every bit we enjoyed watching her hands move very quickly. Then splitting the deck into two in one hand then she flicked the deck back together with her fingers making a loud rap sound, then gave them back to me with a smile and perfect poise.

Denise and I are both very impressed and said thank you.

Denise said would you like to play with us a fun games. Air hostess said I would like to, but I do have work to do. As it will not be long before we start to descend. With a smile, she then walked away. Beautiful could not get any better. As my sister and I begun to deal these lovely well-made cards between ourselves. These cards were silky smooth. Also the quality of a professional Casino deck. The scent of a fresh pack of cards is so lovely especially these. In addition, my sister and I christened them with playing a crude fun game of snap in the middle of the cocktail lounge bar. As you will know, the snap is not a quality game, but it passes the time. However, we were all by ourselves except for the hostesses. Time soon passed the Fasten seatbelt sign was flashing. Followed up by an announcement over the tannoy from the captain.

"We are preparing to land at Lusaka airport thank you for flying with British Airways. on behalf of the captain;" "all of the crew" "we hope that you have all had a wonderful experience and journey with British Airways."

This point our friendly cocktail air hostess came over to us and said that we need to go back to our seats, and you can keep the cards they are a free complimentary gift with British Airways. Thank you very much, and we will remember how you shuffled those playing cards, and we will practice many thanks. Then as asked and as politely, as we possibly could we left the fabulous cocktail bar at 30,000 feet. I hope one day that I would be able to visit a place like this again. As that moment, in my life I really enjoyed this experience.

Denise and I often talk about this memory still to this day. To Making sure that we are, on the correct side of the plane for our seats. As we approach the curtains. The air hostess held open the curtain. Beckoning us through with a bright smile, as we went through the first set of curtains. An air hostess escorted us to the next round of curtains where the same thing happened with another air hostess in the same manner as if the same person trained them. Then passes us on to the next air hostess just the other side of the curtain just like a relay. They accompanied us to our seats in plenty of time. As we arrived at our seats, Amanda was looking out the window, with her hand up to her face as if she was biting her nail. Amanda turned around and said with a concerning tone I was worried about you two the time when the seatbelt sign came on I wondered where you had gone. They do not have parachutes on this plane do they Amanda joked thinking the worst. (With a smile) Showing that she was happy to see us back safe. Then said. "What have you two been up to?" "Well," "it was fabulous it was fabulous it was fabulous this is all we can say fantastic." Then suddenly we felt the plane starting to tilt forward quickly making sure that our seat belts are nice and tight. We looked out the window first of all it looked a little bit like a Desert with patches of green grass and trees, Then suddenly we seeing roads and tops of posh houses with swimming pools. We are not too far away from these luxurious houses. There were shantytowns, suddenly there hundreds of them. Some with wriggly tin sheeting all rusty and Brown and dirty we can just about make the people out. As we flew over they just look like ants, we must be still very high nevertheless we are approaching land. We started to feel that the airplane is slowing down slightly, still looking out of the window we could just see fields of green it was entirely unexpected as I was expecting to see Desert and Dusty Brown. On the approach to the airport, this is so exciting, as we are descending from the heavens.

Moreover, ears pop it is quite a pleasant feeling. Better than the feeling when they are pressurizing the cabin. Suddenly we can hear so clearly just by wobbling my jaw a little bit more to make my ears the plane was slowing. Even more the excitement was starting to build. As the Boeing 747 was smoothly but always slowing down, as we are getting closer to the ground, we can hear the wing flaps motors, we watched them extend the ailerons out of the window. Little bits of missed came over the aircraft's wings as we are using the air to slow the plane down. I explained to my sisters what were the ailerons doing slowing the plane down. Then another three bumps one after each other: you could just feel this through the seat of the aircraft. As the undercarriage came down and locked into place. I could just imagine what was going on in the cockpit. As I am sitting in my seat at this precise moment, everything is going to plan I think. However, we are still Still knowing that we are at the total mercy of the pilot. I have every confidence in Captain Neil McCarthy. Then suddenly the plane began to tilt upwards, and you could hear the wind, as it got very noisy in the cabin I looked around to see what other people are doing in the center seats.

One lady was gripping the arm of the chair with her head right back with a very scary expression on her face. She looked like that she was going to pass out. At a minute then suddenly she grabbed her husband hand without looking at him; hear eyes looked to be fixed to the ceiling of the plane maybe she was praying I felt. Then suddenly as quick as a moment. My Tummy turned over as if I was going over a bridge unexpectedly, what a peculiar feeling it was (but nice). The plane seemed to quiet down considerably. Then suddenly a little jolt rumbled through the cabin as the wheels touched down on the runway; I sank into the seat as mentioned above it was like floating down on a cloud. Then the nose touchdown. (With another little squeak.) The engine started to raw slightly at 1st Then increasing in ferocity and sound as the pilots pushed the engines into reverse to slow the plane down. Tons of metal and people just touched down safely at Lusaka airport as smooth as silk and a seamless as the morning sky.

There was a big cheer from everyone clapping and smiled, and noise of people chatting about that experience filled the cabin of this magnificent plane. The woman that I was watching crossed her chest and then kissed her hand just as if she was praying. I do believe this prayer came true. I thought, thank you father for being there with us all in a moment of need including this lovely lady me am sure that she prayed for all of us.

We taxied for a while. Looking out of the Windows, we could see many other Airplanes all lined up in rows. The sun was dazzling there were A few people on the taxi lane guiding the plane into the park. There was one funnyman looked like he was waving table tennis bats around I think this was assisting the pilot to bring the aircraft into the correct parking space safely. The engine is powered down. We could hear this, and the captain announced that we had landed. At Lusaka airport, there was another cheer from passengers, and the captain said welcome to Lusaka airport, please sit still for a moment while the air hostesses prepare the plane for disembarking.

We can feel the fresh warm air coming into the aircraft as the beautiful air hostesses opened the doors. The seatbelt sign came off, and we are now! Allowed to move freely around the cabin. Everybody was jumping up out of their seats to get their baggage. From the overhead compartments. Everybody was very busy doing something including my sisters, and I. We all formed an orderly queue. Followed each other To the exit doors of the plane; meeting a few friends that we have made on this journey. This airplane as we followed the massive queue. Out of the doors saying goodbye to the air hostesses and saying that we hope to see you soon on our return to the UK Thank you very much for your help and support. You are welcome they smiled, and my sisters and I walked beautifully to exit the plane. The sun was dazzling, and I have to squint. The heat suddenly hit us as the warmth of the air felt fabulous. Taking a moment to the top of the gantry, and we could see Lusaka airport, not a very pretty building as it was just made out of concrete it was not fancy at all. Taking one step at a time and following everybody down the steps onto the tarmac.

I could feel the heat of the tarmac through my shoes the smell in the air of the high-octane fuel was lovely. We all lined up in single file and walked to the airport terminal building. Where we were, greeted by a welcoming committee dressed in traditional clothing of Zambia clapping and singing a native song. It was an excellent welcome; their clothes were brightly colored, and they were jubilant to see us with the rhythm of the music that was very catching just by clapping their hands and singing. Then we walked through a double set of glass double doors into the cooling shade of the airport terminal building. There was one man sitting at a table looking at our passports as we walked in, all we had to do to show him that we have a passport. Behind him was an African soldier looking quite aggressive with a machine gun. The man at the desk was not even bothering to look at the photograph or the details inside. Just make sure that we have one. He did not look too happy, in fact; he looked rather bored. As hundreds of people walked past him not stopping for a moment just a flash of their passport. As he waved them through. Now we have to wait half an hour; we were told to wait for the luggage. Unloaded off the plane. Amanda said let us go and find somewhere to sit before we have no seats. Then suddenly a woman appeared do you have your ticket ma'am she spoke to my sister Amanda. Oh yes, here we go Miss. The woman just takes one look at the candy red and white Stripe tickets and said Miss West and family, please follow me. Moreover, she just turned around and started to walk off, not even checking if we were following. We followed her Quickly for about 200 feet. Into another area and She showed us where to go to pick the bags up and then presented us some seats and told us to wait there until we see the baggage carts appear. Through that door. So explicitly what we did we sat and waited. The trolleys are just taking forever to come. Everybody there just seemed like they were working at their pace. Uncomfortably we were not alone, but it certainly felt like we were. We all sat together on the chairs telling Amanda, about our experiences in the cocktail lounge. Then suddenly we heard a loud crash! Bang! As the doors burst open Nearly coming off the hinges, this long train of carts came through at speed with a man (on the horn) driving it, smoking a cigarette at the time. If anybody had been standing there in front of the door, someone undoubtedly would have been run over, as there was no marking on the floor to be aware of the clear and present danger. An accident is waiting to happen. He drove cockily with no idea of security or safety to others you can say without due care and attention. He turned the vehicle around in a big arc still at speed as people struggling to step out of the way. To make way, as the man halted. He did not even pull the handbrake on! The baggage vehicle trolley train all chained together behind him as he stopped, and the trolleys just crashed into each other as he stopped. Another push on the horn and a wave of his hand To the passengers to collect their baggage and then he jumped out of the vehicle cabin, instantly just walking away with a swagger.

Everybody who was waiting for their luggage stepped forward to grab their own bags suitcases and belongings of the trolley. Checking the bag labels. Before we knew it, we were behind a huge queue of people. There was no real organization there at all. No, health and safety. If we did not hold hands, we would have been lost in the crowd. What are we looking for Amanda, I asked. We are looking for blue bags and brown suitcases. Okay, let us start to see what we can find. Denise shouts outs I have found one. That is great it was Denise's suitcase. 20 min later still looking. Nearly all of the bags are now on the trolley so where are the rest of the suitcases. Then suddenly I spotted something under a canvas tarpaulin at the end of the cart that looked familiar. It was my bag. In addition, Amanda's was next to it. Wow, that is close we all thought. As the driver hopped back onto this truck and started to pull away obviously, that was an attempt to steal our bags. Wow! We have to take our suitcases to the departure lounge. With no trolleys as they have all gone. Oh, dear, which ways it? The building was enormous. Not as big as British Airways in the UK but still it was large enough to get lost in this terminal. There was nothing fancy about this building. Bare concrete floors and bare concrete walls. There was nothing unusual to see. Therefore, what we did in the end was just follow the rest of the people and prayed that they were going the same way as us. Yes, before we knew it, we managed to find another office. After Carrying pushing and pulling this heavy luggage around with us. It was hard work as all the bags and suitcases were hefty and full. Finally, a friendly face, "yes," "May I help you," she said. As we approach, Amanda said, "we needed to get a connecting flight to kiteway airport." The lady says, "may I see your tickets," "please." Amanda pulled out the candy red and white striped tickets from her travel bag.

The woman at the desk looked at them as if she had never seen tickets like this before.

Amanda looked round to us with a worried look on our face "oh dear she said quietly."

Then the African lady behind the counter.

Decided to call somebody else over. By shouting something in their native tongue across the room. Some people that she had shouted over did not know anything about these tickets either. Now we are starting to be scared. Then suddenly the lady that showed us to the seats in the beginning when we landed. Came over and said "hello, please come with me."

the lady is escorted us to another lounge area. Apparently again did not have any chairs or anywhere where we could rest our feet?

"Just wait here for a few minutes," I will pick you up later to take you to the aircraft." Excuse me miss," Amanda asked what plane are we going on." "You are going to Zambian Airways flight 762- kiteway airport," "where you will complete your destination."

Spoken in broken English. Okay, Amanda said. "you might ensure that we are on the plane." "It is not my job to do that."

The woman said. "However, our ticket needs to be," "escorted as this is stipulated on the ticket." "an adult does not accompany us" "Therefore, you need to make sure that we are on the plane."

Amanda said. "Okay," "I will see what I can do." The African woman said. (And then smiled) (You could state and take this as sarcasm from the lady.) Making us quite nervous. All of the children have a fear that they are an apparent possibility of stranded. The African woman pointed us in the direction of the space of the already large and crowded room and asked us to wait there. She will come back for us later. We waited with our luggage sitting on the suitcases and bags feeling quite worried.

Amanda consulted with us and said "that I am sure it is going to be all right." Denise was quite worried, and so was I. we are positive Amanda was too. Secretly hiding our feelings as a fear of showing weakness and vulnerability. In this strange and unfamiliar environment.

Amanda then asked Politely a Canadian couple what plane they were going on. Moreover, what was their destination? They managed to say Zambian Airways flight 762 kiteway airport we all heard that suddenly everything seemed so much better. Instead of worrying, we can just sit back and relax a little bit more this time. The Canadian couple looked charming they had only just got married a few days prior. They were spending their honeymoon on safari. These beautiful couples were very interesting to talk to and told Amanda how they met. Amanda told us later it was just like greased lightning as they were both college students when they 1st met in the summer holidays, and they have been in

23

a relationship ever since. Only just last year he proposed, she was over the moon and accepted his proposal quickly. The solitaire diamond rings were concealed thoughtfully submerged in her champagne glass and a very romantic restaurant in London.

Amanda seemed to make two great friends they just seem to hit it off with them. While they were talking, I decided to have a little walk around. I tapped my sister on the leg, pointed in the direction that I was going. She looked at me then nodded okay. Do not go too far. I just walked to what looked like a small shop, with lots of handmade things in there. Made out of copper malachite somebody told me that it was African art. Board from looking in this shop, I wondered out and walked to some doors where I could see the planes. Then suddenly two soldiers jumped out and pointed their guns at me. I froze instantly. Moreover, then turned around quickly walked back the other way. I had been in a place where I should not have gone. I did not think that I was doing wrong. Nevertheless, when I got back, Amanda was in a panic again thinking that I had been, kidnaped!. As I am only a young boy. However, I told Amanda about the Army soldiers. She said you had better not say anything to anybody. Keep your head down here. You need to stay close to me. I needed to find a bathroom. Therefore, I asked Amanda gain if I could go to the bathroom; she pointed me in the right direction where the toilets were. In addition, said you had better come straight back. I went to what I thought was just a regular gentleman's toilets everything just looked so different there were not your urinals. Just toilets with cubicles. The smell was horrible; as I was in a cubicle, I could hear noises in the next cubicle but did not sound good. It sounded like somebody was in pain. I did not like the place where I am now. I just want to get out. Therefore, I left the cubicle after doing my business as quickly as possible made my way back to my two sisters. Another flight must have landed as we could hear the greeting song of the Africans welcome to Africa sending their song in a beautiful rhythmic fashion. It was quite catchy as I walked back from the toilets; I could feel the rhythm of the music playing in my soul. I started to dance a little bit while I was walking. I watched half an African man on what looked like a skateboard pushing his self with his hands across the floor as if he was paddling. This poor man is disabled, as he did not have any legs. I felt quite sorry for him, but he seemed happy as he was rolling along the floor through the airport terminal with skill and speed. There were many different types of people there I cannot start imagining to show you how busy this airport was. It would be very difficult if one of us got lost as we do not speak the language. However, most of the airport staff do know a little bit of English so at least there was some comfort there. Another few steps and I am back in the place where my sister was? Where have they gone? Lucky enough the Canadian friends that Amanda has met earlier. "We are looking after the luggage." "Hello, Tom" with great welcoming smiles. They both said, "your sister had gone to the toilet," "and she will not be long you must wait here until they get back." "I understand you very much." Feeling some rather the comfort, that there was someone there watching over us. The two Canadians were not paying too much attention to our luggage as they were more interested in their cells. Need I say more than the newlyweds need. Moreover, there was much kissing involve. (Heavy petting) Holding hands and things like that. A little bit of romance in the air (or should say quite a lot) moments later Amanda shows up. "Where is Denise?" "I thought she was with you Tom," "know! Sorry" I said, "I thought that she was with you Amanda." Oh dear. Amanda starts to panic. Then suddenly. Denise turns up with a smile on her face "I found a lovely duty-free shop."

Amanda says, "why didn't you tell me where you are going?"

"We started to panic thinking that you remained lost." "Sorry, Amanda." "However, the shop is only over there." You could tell Amanda was being quite stressed, with looking after two juveniles. The noise came over a crackling tannoy. "Crackle crackle." In addition, we heard just a couple of numbers.

"Oh," "Dear is this our flight, is this our connection?" "What is going on?" The Canadian man said, "weight here I will find out." he went off it must have been a good 15 to 20 min before he came back. "Yes!" that was our flight." "they are holding the flight for us." "We must go let us go this way Please" "Immediately please follow me." We grabbed all our belongings and luggage. Then began to follow the Canadian man. With his new wife. They walked quite fast; it was difficult to keep up. However, it seemed like a long, long way to go. Not like the British Airways airport when you are standing on their passenger transporting conveyor belt to take you to your destination. However, this was just a long foot pounding concrete corridor. Finally! We arrived at the destination meeting a gorgeous African lady and gentleman. At the departure gate. The helpful gentleman assisted us with our baggage. Wrapping labels around the handles and throwing them onto a trolley. Just behind a typical table. They spoke clearly in very good English "you are over an hour late we had all been waiting for you." "Please," "you must come with us to board the aircraft." "As quick as possible," please' "we need to hurry!" "There is no time left to waste," more walking we have to go quite far, at some stages we did run a little bit. It was a lot easier without the heavy luggage then suddenly we have seen the aircraft, Oh dear. It was a big old prop aircraft quite a dirty one; it is looking a little bit battered.

It is not a shiny airplane. We have Never seen this before. No wonder they were hiding this airplane around the back of the airport. It even had a dent in the nose, not a small dent it was a big one I mean a big one. It was a mess. Quite embarrassing to be seen boarding it. All of us walked up the steps gingerly. The African air hostesses welcomed us on this airplane. On to a timeworn aircraft. Inside everything just seemed to be not very clean, just old. Ripped or threadbare. Clearly lacking the maintenance this aircraft deserves. They took us to our seats there was just one Gantry straight down the middle of the seats. Three seats each side six abreast. We sat down after finding our seats there was many eyes looking at us as we were the ones holding the plane up you could tell, but everybody was not Happy with us.

On the other hand, was it just that the plane was a death trap. Causing a massive delay Before we even sat down, we could hear the doors closing, and the engine started to turn. Sitting down and buckling ourselves in the seats. Amanda said, "well this is a lot more different to the other plane." "One Thing previously we are completely spoilt from the last aircraft Tri-Star Boeing 747." In addition, you know what, I am in agreements with my sister. Thinking to myself that this plane is ready for the scrap yard (keeping this to myself as I do not want to panic my sisters) Oh dear it is starting to move. The captain comes over the tannoy in a broad African voice. First, he spoke in Afrikaans. Then he spoke in English. The English surprisingly was very good. The captain said; "we are going to be flying at 25,000 feet," and then the tannoy started to crackle, crackle, crackle, we could not hear anything. For the noise. Then we barely heard the captain speaking. "thank you for flying Zambian Airways" crackle, crackle, crackle. That was a bit backward Tom said, Denise said "what do you mean backward. Well," "we haven't even taken off yet, and the captain is already thanking us." "How bizarre!"

The plane started taxiing in the direction of the runway. It felt smooth. While this was happening, I was looking around The cabin The newly noticing and recognize the lady sitting opposite us on the last plane. She was sitting directly opposite us this time. In a place right by the window with her husband, and a skinny man whom I have never seen before. the couple was in the Boeing 747 that was flying last time. I felt some rather comfort when I seen her as she was holding her husband's hand. I think if she were going to panic this would be the airplane would be worth panicking inside. It is amazing how your environment changes your feelings. Regarding flying. As I remained mixed with excitement and a little bit of fear. Of the unknown. Because we were not sure if we were on the plane to hell and back or the right plane or not? Occurs this one of those horror z stories unfolding. That just seemed to happen. I hope not thinking too hard about this, to myself. Slowly the plane came to a stop. We looked out he window. At the beginning of the runway behind some buildings, there was an airplane full of bullet holes and flame scorch marks. The plane was in a terrible mess the undercarriage was broken on one side, and the plane was tilting to the right one of the wings with touching the ground. I looked closely; I could see the name Zambian Airways. You could hear people starting to talk. "look at that plane Mummy Daddy in what has crashed daddy." (a young boy called out in the passengers somewhere on the aircraft.) "this aircraft was hijacked! (Zambian Airways) Only last week." It leaves your mind to think. Just a thought if we had been on that plane. Our lives would have been in the hands of some horrible evil dictator. Then suddenly our aircraft began to move my heart started to race with a little bit of excitement and a hint of panic. So did the engines! Louder and louder, they were as the aircraft began to roll slowly, at first these engines sounded very different from the original jet engines. Accelerating the speed, we must have been doing approximately 180 miles per hour as the nose of the plane lifted up there was a little bit of a heavy feeling in our stomachs. As the plane, wings took the weight of a fully loaded plane. The plane just bounce into the air leaving our stomachs behind. I must say it was a very thrilling takeoff. Then suddenly after a few minutes the plane started to do a very steep banking turn to the left and then straightened up then did another turn to the right halfway but what a considerable turn was before. Apparently, the captain did not know what direction he was flying, or he was avoiding something. Alternatively, maybe just showing off.

Two mints later, the seatbelt sign flashes for us to take our seat belts off. Then the air hostesses did their little dance, showed us the emergency exits. We laughed ourselves as this show of health and safety was a bit of a farce. The way the air hostesses did as they transpired not choreographed in time together. One was pointing one way, and the other air hostess was pointing the other way. The other one was looking into a very wrong direction, dangerous. It was so funny (we could barely breathe from laughing) it might as well have been a comedy. Even the air hostesses that were doing the safety maneuvers were laughing at their mistakes. (It just goes to show that these Air hostesses were not professional and not adequately trained) though how serious the safety features ours. Compare to the fabulous British Airways staff.

It was a lovely bright day with a few clouds in the sky but not many. We try to make ourselves as comfortable as possible in the cramped seats. I had managed to get an aisle seat at this time. My sister

Denise was sitting in the middle seat, Amanda at the window seat again. Suddenly without any warning or notice, the seatbelt signs come back on again. In addition, the plane started to shake so violently, and it just seemed like it was dancing in the air. I felt my stomach go over. I did not like this feeling as it was quite rough. In addition, very noisy, then suddenly just as quick as it happened the plane leveled out again, we were smooth flying again. The seatbelt sign came off. Everybody was addressing this with concern. Then the captain spoke over the Tannoy. Apologizing for the turbulence that is about to happen. Mixing of warm cold air in and around mountings and atmosphere at an altitude by wind, which Is Causing clear-air turbulence. That's what we were experiencing during this very flight. Apparently, we were flying over some mountings. One can see them through the windows they are a beautiful, attractive site. The seatbelt sign flashy again for us to take our seat belts off, Amanda said, "I'm leaving mine on!" "You cannot be too safe." She was very serious about this. I had to look to see what the woman was doing, whom I have seen Traveling with us earlier in the last aircraft. She was looking at the ceiling again holding a pillow this time against her chest. Her husband was trying to console his loving wife. (I don't think that she was listening to him, but it, was nice for him; just to have been there giving her moral support to his fragile wife). She was in a blind panic. One does not blame her for having a fear of flying. Especially when Zambian Airways is so despicable. 30 min into the flight. A few moments later, everything seems to have calmed down. After the confusion had passed, the air hostesses are now pushing a trolley down the single-aisle between the seats serving the nervous passengers with an embarrassed smile. Amanda managed to get more of those little bottles. A can of Coke for me please I leaned forward slightly to release the catch on the table mounted in the back of the seat in front of me. The table just dropped down with a massive bang unexpectedly and shook the chair in front of me, I know for a fact that this has disturbed the woman relaxing in a chair connected to my table. As I saw her turn around peeking through the gaps in between the chairs. Therefore, one apologized for disturbing her. "I am not familiar with these flimsy tables," I said I cannot believe that the build quality of this airplane and the table was not even flat. It was sloped and quite tired looking and Grubby. I placed my Coca-Cola can on the table. Not feeling like I wanted to drink it because I did feel quite queasy after the turbulence about 30 mines ago. The air hostess just managed to put the trolley away in the back of the plane. I got up and headed towards the bathroom. As I was walking down the narrow aisle of seats, I have got to hold onto airplane seats headrests as I was walking because the plane was lurching left and right and up and down. It was very difficult to walk in a straight line Comfortably without support from the seat headrests. Not too much but it was not a smooth flight I managed to make it to the toilet just-in-time and cram myself into one of these tight little cubicles to my amazement it was not just a typical bathroom. However, this did smell of new chemicals. Not like the fresh fragrance chemicals that the other plane had. I managed to go to the bathroom, but I had to prop and wedge oneself into the confined cubicle to avoid any aiming problems and embarrassing mishaps. Consequently taken quite of accuracy skill and time. Avoiding the Toilet seat, with one's own desperate Powerful stream. Therefore taking longer than usual before finally zipping myself up. Being jostled around with the uncomfortable turbulence in this confined space making any task to perform very difficult to complete correctly and safely. Then washing my hands in this tiny sink while looking at my face in the mirror, above this blue-green sink. As the plane is bouncing around. Thinking, this is awesome! We are going to Africa. Giving oneself, a happy comfort-supporting smile. In the mirror. Just to alleviate any fear. Giving oneself some Personal moral support. At the same time. Thinking at the back of one's mind, I know that this is a Third World country as one's have been told beforehand from my school teachers and friends. Therefore, one cannot expect too much.

While washing one's hands. After drying them with a paper towel, then using the same paper towel to wipe-clean This very heavily splashed toilet seat then throwing it accurately into the blue water of the chemical toilet. Then there was a knock at the door as there was a queue or so one believes. Just coming one shouted, them thinking!

To oneself next time I am going to sit down on the toilet for a pee.

Just to save the cleanup airplane. Mainly running out of paper towels so early on into the trip. That moment while unlocking the aluminum door from the inside. And vacating the cubicle as clean as one found it. There was nobody there. They must have found another empty cubicle. Why do people have to be so impatient sometimes?

In addition, Deciding just to have a short walk, down the aisle. Back to one's seat. Great, I thought my Coca-Cola was still there. Just do not feel like drinking it yet. Then suddenly out of the blue again the seatbelt sign came on and this time we were heading for significant air turbulence. The seatbelt sign flashed; everybody raced to get their seat belts on. Just managing to pull my seat belt strap tight in time. Pressing the Locking mechanical lever home, I push the button on my seatbelt it just seemed as though I had turn the air turbulence on just like flicking a switch it happened that fast. The entire aircraft began shaking violently, and then the aircraft dropped rapidly from its present heading and altitude. Just straight down not into a dive. But shockingly it just fell from the sky this must have been at least 500 feet in one second, straight down or even further as my Coca-Cola can levitate upwards off the table. I was amazed as I felt my body lift up out of the seat; my Coca-Cola levitated upwards into mid-air. Right! Before my very eyes, I raised my hand to catch the can, my right arm felt weightless. Catching The Aluminum Can in mid-air. Grabbing hold of my armrest with the other hand. to stop myself and my can of Coca-Cola from flying off into the air the cabin thus preventing injuries. It is unusual. Nobody was screaming. There were Bell's and sirens going off. I noticed by This moment while looking left over my shoulder out of the window across my sister and with blond hair was standing up on end, and she was clutching both armrests with her white knuckles. I watched her inhale and then scream at the top of her voice.

(scream!- Scream!- scream and more screaming all around!) I had this in stereo screaming as my other sister sitting on the left-hand side of me was also screaming at the top of her lungs. As the plane was dropping out of the sky down and down, it went. A microsecond past then I suddenly felt the fear get a grip of me. At this point, I felt myself inhaling large volume of air in the midst of inflating one's lungs the aircraft leveled out. These thoughts went through my mind, rapidly. We had fallen through the clouds. One of those big horrible clouds that captain Neil McCarthy warned me so much about, when I visited the cockpit In the Tri-Star. As we are receiving severe air turbulence and the Earth is getting closer. Then suddenly the screams intensified One's sister inhaled to scream. Also, the woman across the aisle was screaming out the Lord's Prayer as loud as she could. As the plane was starting to dive closer to Earth the overhead lockers, all bounce open, and everybody happened covered with the heavy contents. The lady began to pray as loud as she could. Rapidly repeating words of the Lord's prayer. Moreover, do you know what. To this day, I do believe that she saved everybody's life. As this was such a scary moment on the airplane rollercoaster. I managed to find solace and sank to choose in the words that she was saying I found myself repeating them also in my mind. The air hostess at the end of the plane seemed like that she was floating in midair frantically trying to grab something for a moment. Then she just abruptly landed with a thump. As the aircraft started to climb. I felt my body get a very heavy in the seat once again, And the engines started to race loudly as the engine seemed like they were at full throttle. Also, I started to feel sick. Other people were being sick in the sick bags. Like this, the airplane was bouncing around in the turbulence, threatening everybody's lives at the same time. Jostling up and down all went down you hear sirens and bells clanking things were being thrown all over the plane. It was turning into a right mess. Moreover, then suddenly as quickly as it happened the Plane begins to climb again. Climbing as if we were trying to take off again. Amanda looked out the window, screened! Like one Has, ever screamed before look oh my God!! screaming, screaming! One cannot look how close we are to the ground. As the ground was as close as it was when we 1st left the runway panic as we can see individual rocks and bushes appear out of the mist on the mounting. As the aircraft was pulling up harshly, one found the gravity on one's face and body. Passengers can feel there self-sinking deeply into the seat as we were pulling G's, massive G. thinking I was going to pass out. I can see people's faces distorting and people fainting Going all limp. I could feel the blood going into my feet as we were pulling up.

I held my breath; squeeze my chest with my arms with my eye's tightly shot for a second. I thought the Wings were going to snap off with the force of the aircraft vertically climbing at one point.

Oh no is this how it is going to end (eyes opened) one watch rubbish rolling toward us in the aisle between the seats. As the aircraft was still dramatically rising, "watch! Out!" somebody screamed. Now hearing loud screams from the passengers in front of one's seats as if danger was approaching rapidly. Tom turned in the direction of screams looking for the danger and the reason of the commotion. All one could notice was, an air hostess running down the aisle frantically trying to keep their balance. At the same time holding a large bungee cord. Then suddenly one could hear screams! From the seat's in front of him a loud rumbling banging noise at that moment Tom scene clear. Present danger without prejudice is significantly approaching with no real warning! Down the aisle at the speed this looked like the air hostess trolley coming towards us like a runaway train. The stainless steel trolley is whizzing past the seats in front now extremely fast. Tom had just pulled his elbow into safety behind the armrest. Just in time for the hostess trolley approaching fast millimeters to spare each side of the walkway, out of control gathering speed like a bullet. The courageous air hostess frantically tried to grab hold of the runaway trolley then suddenly whoosh a large heavy silver object. Like a stainless steel steam powered guillotine blade Came, Flying past Tom's seat. Whoosh! At least 40 miles an hour was an understatement. Narrowly by a hair missing one's elbow. Tom could feel the air pressure change Moments after passing his seat. Followed by a desperate air hostess as the trolley crashed into the back of the airplane where the trolleys are supposed to be parked There were explosions of fizzy pop can drinks. You could hear them exploding bottles and cans fizzing liquid in the steel trolley. Now everybody is panicking. As the plane starts to level out, but the turbulence is still rocking the plane. Up and down bouncing left and right up and down right and left it just kept on and on with the turbulence. While the frantic air hostess run down the corridor of seats with a bungee in her hand securing the hostess trolley as soon as possible; I think that this woman deserves a medal. She is very brave. As the turbulence was bouncing around losing her footing several times while trying to get the hostess trolley securely fixed and fastened so that it would not move and cause more injuries. There was no stopping it again if the airplane decided to do another nosedive. Equally. If the trolley is not suitably secured this will roll straight into the cockpit of the plane smashing through the door then endangering the pilots' lives and the effect of this would have killed everybody on board. Nevertheless; this bold air hostess struggled with her against all odds to save others and to protect everybody on this plane. With the one brilliant valiant attempt to pull in the loose hostess trolley. As she made, it to the tush of the aircraft and tied the rogue hostess trolley off with the bungee safe and strong. Then suddenly the plane level out and it went all calm. Here must have been the end of it, so we all thought. Then suddenly there was a loud clatter bank, and the air masks drop from the ceiling of the plane and everybody just started nervously laughing

In accession, so many mixed emotions were on the plane at this moment. With some calling out with people Fighting to get the masks on their faces as fast as possible, along with the aftermath of a blind panic. A clear plastic tube attached to a yellow plastic mask attached to that expanding clear plastic bag. Tom looked around the cabin left and right making sure that everybody has their mask on, after putting one's mask on first for safety reasons. Seeing the lady who was crying and praying, earlier looked straight at me. She said to Tom "Thank you." To me. I was there that were for a moment, holding my can of Coke in my hand. One was, and she was amazed that we were all still alive. In addition, my sisters were safe and sound, and we consoled each other by holding hands with my sisters.

One said these words to Tom, we believe in you and thank you for praying for all of us. In addition, she said one also believe in your son. We both smiled at each other this is the first time that I had Ever seen this lady smile. Suddenly then her husband sat up after being in the crash position with his face buried deeply into the pillow. The seatbelt signs turned off after approximately 35 min after the beginning of this terrifying little roller coaster ride, from hell on Zambian Airways.

That little rollercoaster ride lasted for about 35 min, but sheer terror adorned every passenger on this flight, from hell! One thinking to oneself at least 50% of everybody on that plane in those few minutes was using the sick bags for one reason and another. I thought to myself and thanked God that the baby was not on board this airplane.

We must have fallen out of the sky at an amazing rate at one point.

As Amanda a said that we were so close to the ground, it must have been at least 500 feet from the Earth. What could make a plain do something like this I just remember what Neill McCarthy mentioned before?

The pilot of the original first flight of the Tri-Star. The Zambian Airways flight was not very comforting in any way shape or form. As everybody was moaning, how this tragedy could of happen. How could one describe the terror that unfolded in a split second while we were on that the

Zambian Airways aircraft, sufficiently enough to explain how bad that moment was. At least the pilot managed to save our lives.

We, however, have about 15 min left of the flight and me, and my sisters start a to play cards. Amanda taught us how to play knockout whist. Was a very interesting game of cards, as we had to make trumps also different hands; so many cards and win hands from other masses. It was a riveting game. Therefore, the time soon went past. And we were just in a moment when we wanted this airplane journey to end, as shortly as possible. So we kept ourselves busy with this card game. Amanda was brilliant at the game she kept on delivering the goods, hand after hand. Over Tannoy, gain crackle,

Crackle this is your captain speaking. Everybody instantly booed. I can barely make out the sound of the captain's voice over the unhappy passengers. During the badly serviced Tannoy announcement, combined with the hollering of the in-flight passengers showing their discomfort and annoyance of a close shave from death. While we are approaching the airport landing strip. Oh, my God, one thought That was such a close shave. Tom thought to oneself that he should never use our fathers name in vain. Nevertheless, we have to land; we cannot stick around up here all day. Especially with this terrible pilot. Therefore, seats in the upright position, seatbelt on extremely tight. At this moment, however, here we go no turning back; we are committed, and it is out of everybody's hands except the pilot. The air hostess looked at everybody's seat belt to assure if it sufficiently tightened. One can say that the air hostess did not find one single seat belt undone on that trip, especially on the approach to the Zambian landing strip. This joke of an airplane started to slow down considerably. Ascending closer and closer to the airport landing strip. The passengers became quiet, and there was an eerie silence over the airplane passengers.

We felt the undercarriage go down a few minutes later on approach to the runway strip the plane flew over the fields. A sick feeling came over me as an approach to the airport was not very smooth at all. It just felt like we were going over a humpback bridge. Along with a small roller coaster, then the plane bounced onto the runway with a screech of the wheels the nose of the plane came down with a heavy thump and slammed into the runway. Then the airplane took off and landed again. People were saying we were bouncing down the runway. We can hear the passengers screaming Just before the deafening noise of the engines. As they are forced in reverse so slowing the plane down the passengers on the plane and me slid forward in our seats, as the plane engines were struggling to slow the plane sufficiently. As we continue now committed to land at kiteway airport. Prayers called out from the lady. Sitting in the seat opposite to oneself, she was also glancing over at the air hostesses with the sheer terror on her faces with a white-knuckle ride one's sister Denise shouted out. Bounce when the airplanes up into the air then immediately back down again. When, will this terror end I thought. I could see my sister's face with her eyes screwed tightly shut in total fear. Here is not the way it should happen one thought to oneself. The air hostesses also looked so scared with the expressions on their faces it just seemed to accentuate the fear on the airplane. Bounce again moved the plane skidding screeching noises from the tires. The rumble of the engines as they are frantically trying to slow the aircraft down. We can feel the tension on the plane as we were holding our breath. Looking out of the window watching the field next to the runway rolling by ....*The airplane managed to slow down to a walking pace although it seemed like an age. Then taxi to a small breeze block building. We waited as three men pushed a set of ladders up to the airplane and the captain announced over the tannoy that we could disembark.

The captain did not have to say this twice. Nobody was leaving the plane; that was not shaken up from the experience but lucky enough still alive with no injuries that I saw. Except for one of the air hostesses who were seen by others and oneself levitating in the middle of the horrific moment, caused the turbulence. She was wearing a big bandage on her knee, sitting down resting her leg. I spoke to her "I was sorry to see that you have injured yourself, I hope you get well soon." I said in a sympathetic voice. With a big smile from her, she said to me thank you for your kind words and smiled again and then said please mind your step. Once again getting out of the airplane that heat was tremendous it was just like stepping into a sauna. We walked down the rickety steps back onto the African soil. The edge of the tarmac just ran onto the red colored dirt.

Then one noticed a white engine racing round to the rear of the aircraft. With loads of trolleys on tow behind the tractor. It was looking like a long snake. (a baggage train) The baggage people there seemed a little bit more switched on. As they worked very hard and fast to get the baggage on loaded. They were just throwing it out of the back of the plane, catching it, and sticking it back on the trolley train. "we are now out in the bush," I heard someone say. My sisters and I walked in single file with everybody else that have been on the airplane journey from hell to a small concrete building on the edge of the tarmac. Everybody qucued to show their passports one by one; passports handed To this grey-haired gentleman who was sitting down behind a glass screen smoking a cigarette. The room was quite full of smoke that he was sitting in you can see the smoke curling up from his cigarette.

His cigarette was hanging precariously out of his mouth. With a large amount of burnt cigarette ash hanging just waiting to drop. As Tom's sister, Amanda passed the passport through the opening in the glass window. The gentleman took these passports and opened it. Browsing with interest at the photograph. While tapping the rubber stamp, on the dry ink pad.

With a rapid, aggressive movement of his arm. He smashed the rubber stamp into the passports with sudden aggression one by one. As he did this, the big curly gray flaky cigarette ash fell. Bouncing off the back of his hairy hand landing on one's own, sister's treasured passport with one sweep of his hand He brushed the dirty ash from the passport. And closing it carelessly then passing it back through the slit in the window without saying a word. Still With the dead but end cigarette still in his lips. Immediately after Handing, the passport back to one's sister we all wanted to have a look at the marks on each of our passports seriously interested. It was a blue triangle. I mentioned we had flown all this way just to get that little rubber stamp making a bit of a joke. We all laughed.

Aforementioned broke the ice while we waited as our baggage is coming off the plane.

Amanda went to a small phone booth to make a phone call. To our father.

(One's sister Amanda Needed to tell him that we were at the airport and that we have all arrived safely.) The arranged airport she was slightly worried because she was not sure that this was the right airport.

And my dad helped her to calm down a little bit and said that he won't be long please sit tight, don't go anywhere with anybody until I arrive.

Then Amanda said, "see you soon dad" then she placed the phone receiver down.

Denise and I raced forward to say something to Dad; the phone already placed back down on the receiver.

This upset feeling came over me knowing that I missed a chance an opportunity to say something to my father.

Amanda said don't worry less you speak to him on the phone the faster he will get here to pick us up. There was nothing inside this airport really. There was nowhere for shops. There was just a little tap on the wall for water. A couple of chairs that were all taken. We waited over 40 min for our luggage to arrive. Suddenly with no warning it's just turned up. On a trolley pulled by a small man. This steady grey-haired old man with no shoes on pulled the trolley straight into the corner of the building, everybody buzzed around their baggage picking and collecting their belongings. In a semi-civilized manner a lot of pushing and shoving and elbows, one remembers this well. The Building comprised mainly made of breeze blocks. Aforementioned painted building must have been over 30 years Old. With for stripes green, red, black and gold with what seemed to be a picture of an eagle.

After doing everything imaginable.

To pass the time, twiddling thumbs shuffling feet feeling quite grumpy as the children felt like they were in a cell not allowed to go out but to stay inside the building. At this moment, a man walks through the door at the far end of the building. We all stood up; went to greet him but no It was not Dad. It was a very sad old man just walking into the building of no consequence in connection to us in any way shape or form. In addition, he just walked past us not even looking in our direction. When is dad going to arrive, when is he?

It was starting to get dark so it must have been approximately 5:30. The baggage came, and we all had to grab bags off the trolleys. A thrilling experience is seeing new places and meeting new people. However, when you are tired after a 16-hour flight and the end of a total 24-hour journey. You do not seem to be very happy to make polite conversation with just anybody. Sitting and waiting for the luggage. Seemed too much like hard work. Nevertheless, it had to be done because if we had left this treasured luggage unattended somebody would have taken it. (for it would never have been seen again) As we weighted for our father that we kept the luggage with this at all times. Another man walks through the door the sunlight was shining on him, and we thought this was just another man. Suddenly we recognized him it's father. He held his arms out to greet us along with the biggest smile that we have ever seen. We all ran over to Dad cuddling him. Kissing him as much as we could, this was fantastic! Memorable Welcome to Africa! I've missed you so much my children! It is like a dream seeing you here. Our father spoke to all of us. With a beautiful calm voice that you can look up to. to all of us full of tears of joy!

With the effects of jet lag plus the turbulent journey of the last flight seemed like nothing, as it was all worth it to see our father once more. For the first time in 11 months. We love you daddy! "we all love you," the children all said it together nice to see you again Dad. Come on children let's not stop here a minute longer let's get the bags in the car and get you all home safely. Oh yes, smiles and happy feelings to all the children. Now the rules are dad said do not let anybody get hold of the luggage. What for I asked.

Amanda said they might steal them. We went out toward the car park carrying the luggage there were lots of kids outside I help you carry bags. No, we will carry them ourselves I help you carry bags now. Kwacha, kwacha! The young boy shouted.

Dad put his hand in his pocket and peeled out a note from inside his pocket. Then Hands it to the child the child walks off in front with the 1 kwacha note and stops everybody pestering us as we were walking over to the car. A five note is worth one-week wages dad said to us. I said you should have given him a 10kk. Right, the car is loaded, and we are on everybody says boggled in the car. Can we open a window dad? No son we have to keep the windows closed until we are moving then you can open the windows. Okay. I said. We drove away from the airport in a white Fiat with lovely Red leather interior. It did not take is too long to get to the house approximate hours worth of driving. Therefore, that's why dad took so long to meet up with us. As he had been now an hour before. In addition, heard that the plane remained delayed, so he left to do some work and then to come back again. We could not stop talking to him all three children saying their bits. Telling him how much we missed him telling him how much we were looking forward to seeing him.

Dad looked very brown, and he was wearing a white suit. This suit reflects the sunlight and keeps you cooler. He says, so I'm glad that your mom has bought you some nice white clothes. Oh yes, she has. By the way how is your mom.

Mom is fine, and she sends her love but she did it in secret so Peter could not here. She told us to tell this to you.

Amanda passes the message on. At that moment we turned right down the avenue of trees; these are called bower-bob trees they are beautiful full of purple flowers and hummingbirds fluttering around the trees. They look like little darts flying around. Down each side of the tarmac road, there are extensive trenches; these are rain ditches.

Dad said. In addition, you must stay out of there because that is where the snakes live. Snakes one said. Yes, snakes they are all types here and most of them if not all of them are poisonous. So, if you get near a snake make sure you get away from him faster, and he can see you. Alternatively, don't even go in a place where you think the snake will be. I understand daddy I said. Amanda said what the address was. Pleased dad she said. Quickly replying father said 14 Maputo AV. Well, that's a nice name and said suddenly we turned round the corner, and we came to a large brick wall with glass running around the top and to massive steel gates in front of it. A security guard is standing there with a truncheon smoking brown papers roll up. Suddenly seeing and recognizing my dad's car throwing the cigarette down on the floor and walking towards the gates coming to attention saluting and then began to open the gates. We drove all the way from the garden and then parked the car underneath the carport connected to the house;

Father rolled the car forward, so the two front wheels went into the ditch purposely. As he parked the car. It was pleasantly cool, even though, the sun was setting, and we arrived under the cover of a sunset. On the right-hand side of the car park, there was a small building dad said this was the house boys house nobody should go in there as that is a privet area for the houseboy only. On the left-hand side of the car, there was a modestly built large bungalow with bars on the windows it looked quite secure. Moreover, it was painted white. With a wriggly tin roof. We unpacked the car and the house with it and helped us carry the luggage into the house. The houseboy the kettle on and started to make a drink he stood in the corner not saying a word as we were all unpacking and taking the suitcases to the rooms. I have my room, and my sisters had to share. At the end of the corridor. I would not say these rooms were overly larch, but they were big enough for what we wanted. Then into the kitchen and we all sat down constantly talking about how we missed that and how much we love him.

Dad was always smiling he looks so pleased to see us everything was going great. We are all at the table now and houseboy serving us a pot of tea. This cup of tea tasted divine.

Father then ask the houseboy to make some cheese on toast. Does everybody want cheese on toast oh yes please Dad we all said?

She settled down quite nicely, in fact. The houseboy started to get the cheese on toast for all of us. Dad showed us the living room. Walking into the living room this was the total length of the bungalow with a dining room attached. Whichever this had made this room very spacious indeed! Most people would say, living/dining area? There was a great oak table with a large umbrella plant Next to the patio doors Dividing the living room from the dining area.

Blinds on Windows that were running the full length of the room beautifully concealing the patio doors. I can imagine that this room. Would be approximately 30 feet long by about 18 feet wide. It was a beautiful spacious room with hardwood floors sparsely decorated with a single sofa four comfortable chairs and a massive fireplace and bookcases each side of the fireplace. With a large lion skin rug in front of the white marble fireplace. Dad explained to us why the mysterious magical cat is called Suttee. How? He got his name. Can you guess? The cat is black and White. This cat likes to get in and out of the living room by a mysterious magical way of which no man can follow. During dad moved into the bungalow. The Cat Came with it.

Dad explained; He could not understand how the cat was getting in and out. He thought that the houseboy was letting him in. However, no; this was not the truth, after long great debates with the houseboy he finally believed that the houseboy was right. Aforementioned is a magic cat;

the Magic cat can walk through walls. Suttee lives in the house. He always has done sins he was a kitten. You see the houseboy believes in voodoo native Black Magic (As it is part of the culture in Africa/Zambia). The Previous owners of the house said that the cat has magical properties, and the magic cat will tell us anything that goes on in the house. So dad, continued with the myth of the marvelous, magical cat Suttee. Just to keep the houseboy under control. At that moment, we turned around, wouldn't you just believe it but as if by magic silently the cat had vanished as if by magic into thin air?

There was no sign of the cat ever been there in the room. As we all looked around the room while sitting down at the large oak dining room table. The myth of Suttee the magic, amazing cat, I will tell you more about him later on. As he turns out to be a very nice friendly cat, a perfect magical pet that a lot of people and friends became envious of such a famous cat. At this moment, the double doors open gently as the houseboy walking in smoothly with a silver tray of piping hot toasted cheese sandwiches along with cold refreshing drinks clinking with ice cubes. Serving us all one by one with perfect etiquette at the table, and then standing back from the table, for a moment with his hands crossed in front of him. Waiting for any orders, from our father.

Dad said, "that would be all for this evening." The houseboy looked around the room in a sheepish way trying to spot suttee the magic cat one so believes. Then steadily in a well-trained way, the houseboy walked out of the room. In a well turned out manner just before leaving. The house boy turned around and stood at the threshold of the doors leaned forward from the waist as if he was bowing to the family, grabbed hold of the double doors handles at the same time. Closing the double doors both together smoothly gently quietly. All this with a perfect pose/posture. We all looked at each other. At the table, dad said we should say grace. Those words of, let's say grace. Are so beautiful. As it has brought the family back together once more. But now there was one of us missing, and it was our mother, thinking, it was a shame that mom was not here to experience this moment. As we, all know that anytime is a good time to thank you to God, for us being here. Father said a beautiful Grace.

Dad always has an exceptional way with words. He is a man of substance that you could sit and listen to and listen. The toasted cheese sandwiches were delicious with just a small sliced onion on them; the drinks made out of cold water and tasted very fruity very refreshing. Have asked us how did you enjoy your trip we explained to dad was an incredible flight it was with British Airways and how lovely everybody was treating us so nice, looking after us entirely, Then, Amanda mentioned how dangerous the flight was on Zambian Airways. As the plane was grubby with lots of broken things aboard the plane on the seats, for example, the tables were falling. In addition, the overhead compartments were difficult to shut and stay close. An old mining Transport system facility. Information had emerged on how Director of Public Prosecutions Mumbo Ichigo and his brother Nchima acquired Zambian Airways. It was pure fraud. Zambian Airways. Did initially called Roan Air. also owned by the then Zambia Consolidated Copper Mines (ZCCM) a parasternal body. Roan Air operated under a company called Mining Air Services. When the MMD government decided to dismantle the ZCCM. A group of people who worked for Roan Air decided to buy the Airline under Management buyout just like the Copper Belt Energy Corporation (CEC) that was originally called ZCCM. Power Division and Copper Net Solutions which was the Information Technology Department of ZCCM. The management buyout (MBO) team at Roan air hired the services of MNB Legal practitioners a law firm owned by the Nchito brothers, Elijah Banda and Patrick Mating the current speaker of the National Assembly. When the time came for him to pay legal fees to MNB, Mumbo gave the MBO team a huge bill. The team failed to settle the bill, and Mumbo Nchito and his partners put Roan Air services under liquidation. What happened from that point forward was a pure fraud because Mutembo Nchito and his brother got Roan Air Services and later re-named it Zambian Airways. The normal thing was to sell the assets. Get the money, not the lawyer Iser acquiring the company.

We were amazed at what dad said, and this is probably why the airport and the airplanes were not up to spec, and the maintenance may be slack. The result of the change of the company's, did you manage to see the airplane that had been shot up at the airport? Oh yes, we did. It was quite scary. We all mentioned as the plane looked in a terrible state on the side of the runway Dad mentioned that this was all over the news only last week; it was quite a scary thought knowing that you would be flying out soon. Like you, all are fathers precious little cargo. Gave a quite a comforting thought. Our father reinforced the idea that he still loves us. We explain to him about the extreme confusion. So, find out how the process of the air hostess levitated in the air caused by the violent air turbulence. Picking her up and dropping her on the floor of the aircraft. She did not stand a chance to grab hold of something even before it happened as she flailed her arms in midair. Frantically trying to grab hold onto something to break her fall. She did not have her seat belt on. She was quite beat. As we seen her after the plane had landed. She was holding, her knee was sitting down with a bandage on, looking not too happy In addition quite embarrassed that she had hurt herself in the turbulence. We added that she was the only injury severely injured person on the plane seriously that we knew. Besides our man that had blue ink all over him. He must have been the man knocked on my toilet door impatiently, moments before the turbulence started. Revenge is sweet. That could have been you in their Tom said Denise, Tom looked down immediately realizing his mistake.

Dad just sat there listening to everything that we had to say. He was quite shocked! You could tell this from the expression on his face, you can see that he was quite annoyed with the air pilot. As a father tends to bite his teeth together, very hard flexing his jaw muscles when he is feeling annoyed. Aforementioned is the only way we can tell that dad is annoyed.

All the same, not with us at this time, not that we normally get in trouble with dad. Then suddenly we noticed another aspect of happiness that none of us happened none of us received any injuries in the air turbulence. Daddy jumped up holding his arms open, stepping forward to give us all a cuddle. You could watch the realization in his face that his children had just been through a rough ordeal. We can sense tears of joy as this household is coming together for all of us including the father. Altogether, it was a touching moment as the tears continued following Down the children's cheeks.

Dad's saying "come children we have got through this we have to gather our strength and be, together as one." "United we stand. You are here now! In addition, you have made it throw hell and back. I promise," "one will do the best in the future to make sure that you do not have to go on Zambian Airways with that horrible, dangerous plane again." "If you are ever asked to fly a plane that does not look safe," "do not get on it. Moreover, phone me immediately I will arrange for you to get onto another flight if this ever happens again your lives are worth everything, Besides you have a fantastic future in front of all." Here was very touching and powerful words from my father once again. At this time, I told Dad that there was a big dent in the nose of the airplane." "this must have caused the turbulence son," my father said to all of us. "The aerodynamics of the nosecone would change making it difficult for the pilot to control the plane."

Moreover, these are the sorts of things that you should look out for, on the plane. Making sure that it is airworthy. These are the same things that the pilot told us captain Neil McCarthy and Tri-Star Boeing 747, as I managed to get into the cockpit of a jumbo jet dad. I said. Wow, you are the incredible young man. The one okay children, dad said is anything else that is urgent that you want to say right now?

No, dad there is anything else that is urgent. Except one thing and what is that children "we love you daddy," a moment of joy flooded over my dad's face accompanied with a big smile. He said come on let's finish your sandwiches and get out that door because we are going out tonight I'm going to introduce you to my work colleagues and friends as they are dying to meet you. Are you all ready yet? We will be leaving for about 15 min, so that gives you enough time to get changed if you need to into some better clothes yes we will dad. I need a quick wash. It only took us a few moments to finish off our drinks and what's left of the beautiful toasted cheese and onion sandwiches. Out through the double doors like a little train of children straight into our rooms and it was a race to get ready.

It was very exciting at the bottom of the bed. As you well know now, we are in a rush quickly what shall I wear thinking to myself and grabbing hold of the suitcase to pull it onto the bed suddenly wish into the air the suitcase flew. Am I Superman or something.

 Is my suitcase empty? I placed the suitcase on the bed flicking the catch is free, and opening the suitcase gingerly at 1st then realizing that the suitcase was entirely empty. A horrible feeling came over. I turned around in a blind panic. And looked straight at the wardrobe behind me the doors slid open and in the wardrobe was my clothes." O" thank! You for doing that. It must have been the houseboy.

He had done the same to my sisters as well and all of the food that was in the suitcases he put them in the kitchen on the table. This houseboy is worth his weight in gold as my dad says. Well, 2 min later we are ready, well, I was anyway at least all I have to do is change into a nice shirt and a pair of trousers for evening wear. Well, we did not know exactly where we were going so the best way to dress was appropriate. One explored the house for a few minutes, as one walked outward the bedroom door the left-hand side was three bedrooms, three doors leading off the hallway a. Four bedrooms in total.

Dad uses one room as his office and is an only bedroom for the self and one bedroom for the two girls. Immediately coming out the right-hand side of one's bedroom There was a square Fourier. Another little corridor is going to the bathroom. Kitchen, opposite one's bedroom door, nearly was the single door into the living room through into the kitchen. There was a set of double doors directly into the dining room area. The kitchen has a massive table in the middle honest one do believe you could fit at least 12 people around this table. The windows in the kitchen sink quite high up but men just being only a young man at this time you can understand that one was only short. I could just about look over the top of the table in the kitchen at this time. There was work surfaces always around and fitted cupboards and a dear friend of the kitchen there was a long stand-up freezer. Next to, it along the stand-up fridge the floors in the kitchen area just seemed like concrete polish to a high standard. I would say probably with boot polish as it is the Africans favorite product of choice if they wanted, something polished. They use boot polish of choice.

Moments later the father comes out straight into the kitchen, "okay Tom what you think of one's house." "one love this dad!" "I can't wait to see the garden in the daylight." "Oh yes." "It's going to be a busy day for all of us tomorrow as we have a lot to do." "What?" I said, "yes we are all going out tomorrow." Through the business," "you're going to enjoy this." "Oh," "the excitement came over, excited about this." "That can be a fantastic holiday," "we are going to be traveling?" "yes!," "Cannot wait for this," Dad said, "Listen Tom don't tell the girls yet." Among us the advantage of its always best to keep a little secret. It's between mean you as a surprise for the girls tomorrow. I understand that I will do my best.

Here come the girls.

Amanda and Denise were both in new dresses, with big smiles. We are ready the girls said.

A little twirl from

Denise and Amanda showing off their new clothes

Dad said you both look beautiful my little daughters, and Tom you look very handsome too. Okay, everybody together let's get into the car. We all walked out of the kitchen door to the carport on the side of the house. The lights came on as we walked outside and let the car up. I wanted to get into the front seat, but Amanda battled and jumped into the front seat. She, usually, does this nevertheless. As Amanda is the eldest, so we must give her the respect that she deserves.

Dad walked around the front of the car after locking the house door, and then walking around the front of the car jumping into the driver's seat and starting the engine.

Dad showed us why he put the front wheels of the car in the ditch, and it was a drainage channel for any heavy rain. He put the car in reverse and said imagining if you are stealing this car then he accelerated to try and get out of the ditch in reverse the car just would not have it however much he tried. Here is an excellent safety feature dad said. Then he drove the car forward a few feet, and then reversed the car again still no joy dad could not get the car to reverse down the drive.

A great antitheft feature built into the house dad said. A person with a black uniform came to the side of the car; so is everything alright bwonner.

This man was a security guard looking after the house.

Father said everything was good. Then dad put the car into first gear; drove forward over the grass around the garden, and around the house straight back onto the drive. Up to the gates, where the security guard was waiting to open the gates. The Security guard opened the gates a little bit and walked outside, looking up and down the street and then proceeded to open the gates.

Dad drove through the gates and onto the main road. He did not stop to make sure the gates were closed we just turned smoothly out and away from the bungalow. As we were driving, through the streets. Dad was telling us the names of the roads and what ways that we would be allowed to go down and what roads not to go down as this is quite a dangerous area. If you have to go out for any reason, you must stay together. Do you know this child? "We understand father. It was quite an intense security lesson for just a few minutes of driving out of the bungalow and down the road. Without telling us directly, we could be robbed at any minute. Possibly, even by gunpoint just because somebody wants what we have whether it is simply just the car or just our money.

"The security lessons are very serious and need to stay practiced this daily," Dad said. "Now anyhow, kids on the brighter side of things, you will be meeting the director of the company." "Oh, the director, yes and partner." "Now when you are meeting him make sure, you are polite and practice your best manners." "When you see him might not think that he is a director, but he is, and he is a very important person and you must give them the respect that he deserves at all times. But to make sure I will introduce you to him. His name is Colin dad said his name out loudly!" 'We all laughed as daddy is a partner of Mitchell Cotts," and he has just told us. Then dads said, "write children we are going out for a meal with one's boss and his wife and other influential people in the business." "So please be on your best behavior." "Where are we going Dad," Amanda said, we're going to a Chinese restaurant down the road from the offices. Chinese I said, what is that."" I have never had Chinese before," '" and it's going to be quite a learning experience," we're now driving through a small tunnel to the town." The roads were not busy at all and were reticent a few potholes here and there. Besides, that though, the roads seemed very smooth, and it was pleasurable drive as the scenery is beautiful all was light-up by moonlight and street lights.

Chinese Restaurant

We will not be long now Dad Said. As we are just about to turn, the corner dad started to tell us about the restaurant "they make fine noodles and dumplings all the dishes made with fresh ingredients with no artificial colorings or preservatives." "In addition, you can eat with chopsticks, Denise said chopsticks what are these it will not be long, and you will find out." "Let me tell you for this is your first visit to a Chinese restaurant." "I would like to explain the Chinese style of serving." "In China," "diners order collectively and share all dishes," "which are served at the table in random order as soon as they are ready." "In this way," "mixing the textures and flavors of the dishes adds to the enjoyment of the meal."

"So please do not allow your dumplings to go the cold while to wait for your soup!" Dad said.

Arriving at the charming restaurant, dad, parking the car in the back of the restaurant. Through some gates; left the car nice furthermore safe we saw two other Fiat cars in the car park that were identical to dads. In addition, there was a very nice big Jaguar. That must be the director's car one thought to oneself we all walked steadily, and we are all welcomed at the door by one of the dad's colleagues. Welcome Jim is this your family. Yes. Amanda Denise and Tom, I am happy to see that you have all arrived safely. "This is a very long way to go just for an" I said, we all laughed. Then our fathers' colleague showed us through into the main dining area and introduced the family to the director. Jim good friend you can sit by me the director said. Children make you feel comfortable, and it is such a pleasure to meet you, we are about to start ordering, I take it that your children have had Chinese before. Know I am afraid not.

Dad said, "this is their first experience with Chinese. Well, they are going to enjoy this evening as it is a special occasion, we need to talk a little bit of business, but the rest is free time to enjoy the meal. What is your name?"

the director said to Mc. "Tom Sir" I replied. "Nice to have your acquaintance Sir." "It's my pleasure to meet you Tom I am the director of Mitchell Cotts Ltd;" "your father is the partner as the papers signed:" "Earlier today Jim is a fabulous asset to our company as he has the skills;" "experiences to bring this company further forward." "Well," "he makes a very excellent father." "I'm sure he will work well with this company." The director smiled one's name is Colin "It's a pleasure to meet you Tom" and "who are these two lovely ladies." "I waved my arm over; said, "these are my sisters."

"Denise introduced herself I am the middle daughter very nice to meet you Colin also knowing that our father does partner with your company makes us all very happy." Don't you agree to look over her shoulder to

"Amanda and I oh yes" we both agreed? "Is there anything that you like on the menu?" Colin said. "A waitress appeared with four menus," handing them out to each of us."

Dad spoke in Chinese fluently to the waitress she smiled and bound and then walked off. A few moments later bringing a tray of drinks in for the whole table. Bowing every time she approached the table and left the table. Aforementioned happened with every Waitress that came to the table. You could see a great deal of respect honor and integrity at this table. It must be something to do with Director Colin of Mitchell Cotts Ltd. As this man seemed to be very powerful, and everybody on the table respected him in every way. They hung on every moment of every word that he said. The table was a large round table, and there was a small table on top of the roundtable this small table would move around and the dishes served at this round table. One was impressed with this particular table as one does love technology I. Colin said, and your name is, young lady. "My name is Amanda; it is my pleasure to meet you Colin." "Know Amanda the pleasure is all mine," Colin said. Dad was smiling slightly; you could tell that he was quite pleased with our actions posture and etiquette at the table.

Dad said, "I know there may be some mistakes and few accidents on the table today, but this is the first time that they have ever experienced Chinese cuisine." We all smiled. One is sure dad said this to back his self up just in case any accidents did happen.

As he has, apologize for any mishaps before they have happened. A good move. I would say the roundtable was suddenly very busy with loads of young Chinese women carrying trays of food to the table; giving us hot towels to wipe our hands-on before we started eating. They smelled of fresh lemons and was very refreshing. We watched our father as he showed us how to tackle the chopsticks. To begin with, it was very difficult, and we all found it hard to get started. Then suddenly Amanda was 1st to pick something up with her chopsticks it was a piece of pineapple. Amanda popped it into her mouth and smiled gracefully. And nodding, to say that she had done it. One was still struggling chasing things, around one's bowl. Then suddenly Denise managed to pick up some noodles and threw them around her chopsticks just like spaghetti Bolognese. Sister also managed to pop the noodles into her mouth. With no mishaps. One proposes from a trained eye. One would notice that Denise has never used chopsticks with noodles before in her life. Therefore, one must say that she's doing extremely well for a novice.

It's things turn now trying one's best with the pork ball, still chasing it around the bowl. By this time, I'm getting rather hungry and impatient with myself for not managing to pick up this pork ball, however, tasty it looked I still could not manage to pick it up. Then suddenly, one had an idea one skewered it like hunting fish in a barrel. Picking this pork ball, upon one's ivory chopstick. Placing it into one's mouth, as one has always been never told to eat off your knife or fork. Oh dear, it's a little bit hot. However, one kept it in one's mouth. One's cheek was full. This pork ball was a delicious one had never tasted anything so amazing and divine in my life before the juices of this delicacy, filled my mouth with tasty explosions of delights. As the mail went on you can see that we were all getting quite adapted to handling these rogue chopsticks. One could feel the muscles in one's hand starting to ake, so one have to swap hands I found it quite easier to eat with the left hand than the right. But still showing of eating with the left and then eating the right eventually by the end of this meal I know that one would be a professional with his chopsticks.

Denise was starting to pick up green beans and place them in her mouth one at a time. She seemed so delicate and professional.

Amanda was just eating with her fingers like a little piglet at the table. No, not, ones only joking she also had perfect table manners. Oh, ones dear Sister Amanda, one day is going to read this book, however, to see what things said about her. It doesn't matter things sure; she'll understand. Course after course Into the room. A particular delicacy served to us. Here the delightfully tasty food is called a spring roll, so sweet looking; delicious that is a delicacy is so interesting. Smelt superb. Tasty Finest spring roll that we have ever eaten ever if we had done served just spring rolls. We would have loved it we all remarked on how fabulous these spring rolls were Denise and Amanda and everybody else actually enjoyed them. We remember them to this day. Nevertheless, one has never eaten in a Chinese restaurant that can surpass. The incredible flavors were in the spring roll. With this food and more food, this was a banquet. Meeting of business was working well for father stayed looking so professional and kept his own.

The other members were watching every move that we made. The best thing for us to do is to Dine. Keeping quiet and not say a word just enjoy everything that is going on around the room. Moreover, the conversation that is apparent around the table. One popped something into one's mouth it tasted disgusting one think I was told that it was raw ginger I really want to spit it out, but I daren't. As this would be shown to be offensive table manners and very rude. With regret, one swallowed it. One could feel grating down one's throat. As one did not agree with the taste Reaching for one's glass taking a large sip of mango juice. One thinks oneself are about full now. The roundtable in the middle was still spinning around back and forth, as everybody was picking out their favorite morsels using their chopsticks. Looking so professional making real business. I heard that Mitchell costs were something to do with mining and something to do with rubber or something to do with copper. These a lot of different things that they were talking about dad was explaining about different rock formations and he was also explaining about water pressures, etc., I noticed one of the ladies was taking notes occasionally so this must have been quite an important meeting. Occasionally one's father lit up a cigarette Rothmans Royals was his favorite and the director Colin also lit up a cigar.

Colin said it's very difficult to get cigars in Africa now as there just seems to be a shortage. One is thinking. That is why one had a large box of King Edward cigars in one's suitcase at home. So now, the penny drops and things start to unravel. In a friendly way, the conversation of business was brought to a close. In addition, we all started to make polite conversation about our enjoyment in Africa. And our first flight. We told them a little bit about the air turbulence also about their air hostess that hurt hear the knee.

Colin was very interested in everything that we had to say. We all agree that he was a very nice man. After the meal, dad pulled out a large King Edward cigar, cut off the tip of one of them, and gave the other King Edward cigar to Colin.

Colin pulled out a silver and gold cigar cutter. Snipped off the tip of his cigar rolled it in his fingers next to his ear, furthermore saying "so this is a fine cigar" dad smiled, as he was lighting a cigar off two matches. Also rolling it in his fingers and leaning back in his chair. Colin was doing the same. Large plumes of smoke wafted over the table as dad and Colin enjoyed their cigars.

Colin asked. Tom, what would you like to do when you are older? One thought for a moment and said. After remembering what Neal McCarthy said, in the cockpit of the plane. One would like to be in aircraft pilot. One's dad was quite shocked. In addition, Colin smiled and said your son is reaching for the stars with his talent as an entrepreneur of his impressive and capable future. One does believe like father like son.

Colin added. Colin asked the same question to one's sister Denise what would you like to do for a living when you are older. One would like to make her perfumes, creams, and sell them as an international business. By using natural elements. Suddenly Colin was engrossed in what Denise had to say about her business future. Moreover, what would you like to do Amanda Collins said? I would like to look after children and be a child-minder one day.

One of the ladies that introduced us to the table at first became very interested in this statement. From my sister Amanda. How very interesting she said. Suddenly the whole table became very interested in what Lynn had to say to Amanda., In relation to child minding. Lynn started to tell us about the courses of child minding; one must add that this is very interesting. Child-minders look after one or more children under the age of eight for more than a total of two hours per day. They do this in a domestic setting (typically their home) for payment. Registered child-minders are inspected by Ofsted in England, or the Care and Social Services Inspectorate (C.S.S.I.W.), to ensure they provide a safe and stimulating environment for the children that they were providing care next. Registered child-minders are, usually, self-employed and run their own business. Some may employ child-minding assistants. Although Every day will be different, a child minder's typical day may include. Visiting a park, museum, library or playgroup arranging fun and stimulating learning activities, such as dressing-up, creative play. Reading celebrating cultural events from around the world providing meals Snacks for the children. Involving them in food preparation and menu choices taking children to and from school or clubs working with other local child-minders to directed group activities. Child minding is a dynamic and evolving career so, once you've got your new business up and running; there are plenty of courses and training opportunities that will develop one's knowledge and confidence. Being part of P.A.C.E.Y. - the Professional Association for Childcare and Early Years - means your new child-minding career will get off to the best start with the best support. Therefore, if you ever need any assistance in this area of expertise, I would gladly assist you. Amanda and Lynn then seemed just to make good friends instantly is there any position for childcare within this organization? Lynn said Colin. Colin said, "we will have to look into this," "As I'm a great believer in looking after the family," "not just the workforce" my father also agreed on this. Colin said "Lynne; I was not aware that you have done so much in relation to childcare." Lynn said, "it was a very rewarding job as I have done it for seven years in the UK." "Impressive!" Colin said. "We will have to look into it," "can you make a note," "Oh yes," Colin, Lynn said. Lynn jotted down on her notepad. A big smile came over Amanda's face as she just seemed to be the star of the table. In addition, dad was very impressed with what just had taken place. "Now that's what I call a natural progression of networking," Colin said. "So as one can see we all managed to enjoy a superb meal and fabulous," intelligent conversation with the added expression of meeting new people. Nobody realized how long we had taken over our meal. As the meal was so delicious however the company was entirely interesting additionally instructing for all

As you can well imagine the night is ending, as there were sneaky little yawns appearing from the children. One thinks it; it's most a combination of the jet-lag. This fabulous food was also keeping such perfect posture for such a long period with the combination of everything that has gone on over the last few days. All three of us start to feel very sleepy. Our father saw this, therefore politely making reservations to justify the family from the table and to make the closure for the evening as it was 3:30 in the morning. We waited for dad to make the first move to exempt us from the table and to excuse us from the restaurant. Dad noticed our signals and not wishing to let one of us fall sleep on the table, for instance. Said to Colin, "I think this concludes our evening." "I must stress that had been a very long day for my children as they have flown 15,000 miles in 24 hours to arrive at this restaurant."

"Jim I understand," said Colin. "It has been a fantastic evening full of interesting conversation and polite Society." "One is proud to announce you as our second-in-command of the directorship of Mitchell Cotts Ltd." "So please take your children home and have a pleasant day with them tomorrow." "we will catch up the day after as it's going to make oneself a day or two to design a brief for the company announcement."

"It doesn't matter who you are," "only what you will become."

"Come on then children lets be ready now." "We said thank you very much" (altogether) "Thank you for a lovely evening you have been the perfect host," "one has learnt so much from this evening," Colin said, to me "I'm glad you have all attained and had a pleasurable time."

Master Tom. Colin it does not matter what you are just what you will become this is more or less what I discovered this evening. Take care Colin I said while shaking his hand. Taking interns with the pleasantries of saying good night. Good night Lynn, I said, to Colin's wife. It's a pleasure speaking to you. Father said: children are we already now. Beckoning us towards the door, through the door and into the car park, we went. We were astounded at the remarkable view of the sky; I have never seen so many stars in the night sky before. It was spectacular I could not believe my eyes, especially when I seen the Moon. One has never seen the moon upside down before.

Dad looks at the moon I said. It's upside down. Yes, my son, that is because we are the other side of the Equator, so the moon looks upside down. You learn something every day don't you son, oh yes dad, furthermore I love it. Looking at the fabulous moonlight night I am so happy to share it with my family for this is an experience of a lifetime. One knows that one can speak on behalf of one's two sisters. They too have had the most enjoyable evening of their lives so far. In addition, the evening isn't even over yet as we still have to drive home. The cool night brings the air so fresh and clean. The only way I can compare it to is after a hot summers day in the mountings when the sun has set, and the stars are out with the wonderful release of mountain air flowing through the town. As an expression of life's small luxuries. All this just walking across the car park in the silence of the night.

Dad opens the car door. One can hear the buttons popping up. Amanda jostles to the front of the car again; it is too late, and we are all too tired. She put up a fight about who's going to sit in the front of the car. Especially in front of Colin and Lynn our hostess for the evening. One must say, it would not have looked good. (An argument in the car park after a fantastic business meeting) Would have just been terrible. We all embarked on the car and found our seats. Closing the doors without winding down the windows as the father had said. How important it was to keep the windows closed until we have started to move. Especially when dad is maneuvering the vehicle at a slow speed around the car park. Aforementioned is when we are at the most vulnerable.

Dad let us know this. A turn of the key and the engine starts up with a raw, smoothly dad reverses out of one's parking space, in a perfectly executed maneuver. In the direction of travel to drive straight out of the gates. We looked around to wave goodbye to Colin. However, they had already gone back into the restaurant. Here is just another safety feature, or maybe they were just having a little debriefed about the meeting with Jim's little family. A smooth drive of the car park through the gates into an adjacent road.

Dad turned very gently before one knows one was fast asleep; Amanda stayed awake, and one's sure Denise did too. One sure it must have been the combination of fresh air also the long traveling has just caught oneself up. Unknown Amanda, Denise, and one's father had a good conversation about the evening that, one totally missed out-on. Telling you this though. It was the best sleep that one had had for a long time. Until the end of the journey when the car had drove in through the gates, one still not awakens, the guard had closed the double gates, and one still did not wake up. The car rolled up the car Port. The security guard closes the gates behind the car dad rolled the front wheels into the drainage ditch. And then started to get out of the car Denise gently stroked my cheek with her fingers, to wake me up without startling me, I woke up pretty much instantly but gently. Aforementioned is such a nice way to be woken up cum on son dad said let's get you into bed, dad carried me from the car into the bungalow and straight into bed. I was fast asleep in moments. So much looking forward to the day ahead of us once sleeping soundly.

All that could hear was the character song of the crickets it sounded a little bit like white noise, but beautiful to hear. It would drown out any background noise.

Dad had placed me into bed when saying "good night son." (Whispered gently into one's ear) "Sweet dreams," then kissed me on the forehead, tucking me in at the same time. Going to bed feeling safe, with a happy inner smile feeling producing cozy warmth of comfort to me, is a contented pleasant feeling.

That any good parent would offer unconditional love.

Unconditional kindness and therefore memories remembered by yourself I hope you remember the Sweet childhood feelings when you were also young ones.

Good Morning

The dawn breaks, with this wonderful, beautiful tropical sunrise. Sun was rising through the window casting shadows from the window bars. Stretching the shadows from the security bars creeping up my bedclothes and gently flooding the room with gorgeous golden light. One could feel the warmth of the golden sun touching once hand as one lay in bed. One was watching the sun smoothly rising rolling up my arm and then onto my face. That room went so bright making oneself squint furthermore turning out to be a beautiful morning, the heat of the sun was so refreshing. The white walls of the small room reflected every bit of sunlight around the walls of the bedroom until this room does become entirely flooded with sunlight. If one were a vampire, there would have been no escape from the bright sun. One thought, one dream. Then remembering the past stories, that Peter had told us about vampires. Shrugging this horror off even though it lasted a moment it still left the strange fear damage to one's feelings. Then rubbing my eyes then stretching my arms up hi. Quickly pulling back the bedclothes immediately sitting up in bed. Glancing over my right shoulder out the window taking in the glorious view of the lush green garden. Then suddenly I saw something on the windowpane; it looked slightly transparent but bright green. I stood up innocently naked walked over to the window to get a closer look. It just looked like a little green frog. Then it started to walk across the glass. Gently snuggled itself into the corner of the windowpane. Oh, so cute, amazing one thought to oneself. Standing there naked in one's bedroom looking out of the window millimeters away from a beautiful tropical frog. The frog licked his nose then his face closing one Jet-black beady eye at a time with his very long bright red tongue. It was effortlessly beautiful and edgy. One of God's most beautiful creatures. One looked past the frog after studying it for at least 10 min. Into the garden, I gazed looking left and right through the window to see what else I could explore. The security guard was sitting on a low wall near the gates but behind the massive exterior wall so covered on the top with broken glass bottles. All different colors of a glass of which were catching the sunlight lighting up like small diamonds across the top of the wall. The security guard was asleep as his head was down and did not seem to stir or move his arms folded across his body. It is about 5 o'clock in the morning one must go out and explore this large fabulous new garden. Pulling one's boxers up and then put my trousers on!

Then stepped into my right shoe, then naturally the left shoe as one, normally, would. Suddenly I felt a lump move in my footwear, so one pushed and stamped harder than usual. Crunch, one felt this in one's shoe. It scared me, a little; instantly one pulled the shoe off. While emptying the unknown contents onto the floor. An ugly looking bug appeared. Its legs were moving, and it looked like it was in pain; it was bleeding, not thinking immediately I hit it hard with the heel of my shoe, and split it went. I saw a small flash of light like a little Ping-Pong ball shootout out of the murdered creature. I felt a creepy feeling all over my body. Shaking an eerie feeling of disgust off with a rapid wriggling movement of my body, saying "yuk." then checking my shoe once more. Before putting it, back on my foot. Making a mental note, to oneself always empty one's shoes before putting them on in the morning. The beetle was a real ugly looking thing. Now it is very dead.

I cannot leave a murdered Beatle's body in the middle of my bedroom floor. As this may be seen by someone and may upset them. Remember; always think about the third person's feelings. My dad used to say. Therefore, for this reason, I promptly ran back into the bathroom grabbing a handful of Easel-tissue paper, off the role in the bathroom. Running straight back into the bedroom, as quickly as I could to clean up the evidence of the murder victim on one's bedroom floor. One must say I did not feel too happy about the murder, of this ugly looking beetle. Some people may say that it is justified, but indeed, one cannot honestly defend this action of death to this poor innocent creature that crawled inside my shoe for shelter. It made me feel quite sad while I was cleaning up the crushed remains of this lifeless body. The contents of the body were yellow. The shell was a golden brown. I know what word is in your mind, and the word is a cockroach, as you can see thoughts can transferred I thought to myself.

All done all cleaned up and flushed away not a very fitting burial. Somebody may say. Nevertheless, it is done now. You may say that one has gone overboard on describing their feelings about this cockroach, but one have to say this was the first ever creature that one had ever killed. Now I have just immortalized my first murder in plain text for everybody to see.

Fabulous Garden

Not thinking about breakfast, just thinking what a fabulous garden, one had to explore and walked gingerly out of the kitchen underneath the car Port shelter now the garden is in full sunshine. Therefore, one can see all of the beauties and splendors and wonders that this garden is holding within its high walls made out of breezeblocks topped with broken bottles of all different cultured glass. The houseboy walked out of his hut connected to the car Port in his uniform. Greeting me with a smile and a moderate bow. He began to sweep the floor with what looked like a handful of twigs but was an African Bayes broom. I smiled back at him turned left and walked into the main garden. A delight of tropical plants stretching out around the edges of the garden, in the one corner a bamboo plantation that was at least 20 feet high and the center of the garden was a medium-high tree. I walked further into the garden to explore even more. A large black bird of some kind flew out of the tree, with long black tail feathers. I cannot tell you how lush and green the beautiful garden looked, but I will do my best. The flower borders were in full bloom. The grass was very green and healthy it was a very beautiful place to be. Therefore, one carried on walking round the garden and around the bungalow walking down the side of the house where there was another large tree. It has some bright green fruits hanging from it. One walked past the tree around to the front of the garden where there was a large yard big enough a five-aside football pitch or even tennis courts. There were no flowers in the front garden. One walked past oneself sisters bedroom window, then my father's bedroom window, then my bedroom window all pointing out to the front of the house along a small running the front length of the bungalow. Then pass the kitchen window to the front carport on the other side of the walls around the garden there were trees growing up and over the top of the wall. Even at the front where the drive ended up under the car Port. It took me a few minutes to walk round the bungalow. The security guard came up the path and said something to me in Afrikaans; I did not know or understand what he said. So I walked quickly back into the bungalow. My dad was in the kitchen making a cup of coffee. Morning Tom father said. With another welcoming, smile. One also said good morning dad, would you like a drink son. Yes, please. He poured oneself a large glass and mango juice, which was delicious. Then asked oneself would you like anything for breakfast? That would be lovely. Breakfast served at 8 o'clock. Going to get ready and one will meet you in the living room. Ready for breakfast. Are my sisters up yet Dad? I said. No, not yet, son but one will give them a knock and tell them what time breakfast is. At that moment, the houseboy walked into the kitchen. Good morning, bowanner he said in Afrikaans, the houseboy said. Breakfast! Said dad. Three children's breakfasts and one adult want continental style. "Yes." "Cum on Tom out of the kitchen let the houseboy do his work." "What do you think of the garden anyhow. Have you had a chance to have a good look at it", "I think it's fabulous dad." I asked is that bamboo in the garden? Tom's Dad said I had made sure that all the leaves were burnt off underneath the bamboo to make sure there were no snakes, so you are free to play in their if you want. That is excellent. Dad walked off down the hallway to the bedroom and knocked on the door at the bottom of the corridor. Shouted out to the girls good morning girls. Breakfast will be at 8 o'clock making sure you are ready. Yes! Father heard two sleepy voices coming from behind the door. Then father walked off into his room. As one walked into the living room. One was hoping to see Suttee. Suttee was nowhere to be seen. One walked over to the patio doors, unlocks them, and opened them wide so one can see the full splendor of the garden stretching out before one's eyes. The large tree in the middle of the garden oneself stood there looking at it for a few minutes. Then one heard a squeal. What was that animal thinking for oneself? Then one has seen that black tropical bird flying through the garden with something in its beak; it looked like a giant lizard. This tropical bird flew over one's head and the roof of the bungalow. Then it was gone! Out of sight. Moreover, all was calm again. Something startled one touching one's leg; Tom froze on the spot for a moment and then plucked up the courage to look down. Revealing a pleasant surprise and then Smiling to oneself, it was Suttee, the cat. Tom put one's hand down to stroke the lovely cat, as soon as Suttee felt once hand on his back. The cat bolted and ran straight back into the garden. Then disappeared into the foliage as if by magic. A moment of connection thinking to oneself now one knows that Suttee and one's Self-are good friends. Like this, the cat has made the first move. Making the early steps towards the beginning of a lovely friendship. Just standing there for a few moments taking in the morning breeze, one could feel the warmth of the day. Growing within his feelings, and the relaxed atmosphere of the garden soon enveloped tom's mind. The garden still did not have a breeze in the air. It was very still in the garden. One was thinking that the tree would be a brilliant place to make a den. On the other hand, even a tree house. A bamboo tree house now that would be exciting. One walked further out into the garden. Plucking up the courage and walking straight into the bamboo. One tried to put once hands around a piece of bamboo. It was too big for my hands to reach all the way round. I tapped it with my knuckles it sounded hard and felt very sturdy but made a nice sound. One caught something moving in the corner of one's eye one turned quickly. On the side of the garden wall was a lizard scurrying around. That caught my eye; one was amazed how agile; nimble this lizard is. As the little creature is defying gravity, scurrying across the wall as if one would run down a footpath on a summer's day. With an expression in Once, own urban environment. This little fellow was cream in color with a very few dark brown stripes down each side of his body. Therefore, one froze on the spot, to use the bamboo as camouflage so one can study this unusual Lizard. In its natural habitat without disturbing it... a little bit nervous at the same time excited to see something that I have never seen before. One should say. Just getting used to the environment, oneself is only a young boy. In this magnificent African garden not knowing what the dangers are. However enjoyable flown halfway around the world with one's sisters to this African continent to visit our father in this tropical environment to oneself, a trip of a lifetime. (Calling from the bungalow) hearing ones sister's call out one's name, "Tom!" "Morning," (To acknowledge her) also to give one's sister some idea exactly where one was. She did not hear the first time. Therefore, she called out again but this time with a little bit of a panic in her voice. Morning Amanda ones in the garden one shouted. The lizard just disappeared. Okay, Amanda says loudly. Breakfast will not be long. Okay. Calling out, "just exploring the garden. "Moments later. One started a steady walk back to the bungalow from the bamboo plantation. The smell of freshly cooked breakfast tantalized one's nostrils and taste buds. As one walked closer to the patio doors. One could hear the radio. Dad was standing next to it smoking a cigarette listening intently to what radio broadcasters have to say. World Service, one heard these words. Here is a fabulous radio station that everybody is talking about, it is filled with entertaining shows morning days and evenings around the world. ('is used as a communicator through the world at 6 AM listen for special broadcasts) (as they will only be announced once')

Father stubbed his cigarette out. Then he said. There you are Tom, in time for breakfast dad said, with a smile. One joined their sisters who were already sitting down at the table. Amanda said one was worried about you. One was just having a good look around the garden once said. Would you like some bacon, Denise offered oneself the plate of bacon, in addition, one started to take off the bacon that one wanted. Egg tomatoes mushrooms beans fried bread. It was all there as a perfect British breakfast. Father turned the radio down slightly and then came to sit down at the table. Then he started to dish out his food. Dad does like a substantial breakfast. After everyone served their selves from the platters in the middle of the table. Father said, "Hands together eyes closed," Dad started to say grace. "Bless this food for the goodness that we are about to receive now we all are truly thankful. "Amen." "You may begin children." The bacon tasted delicious so did everything else. Dad pointed at his coffee cup; the houseboy poured out father a cup of coffee, then proceeded to pour the children, Orange juice.

Dad spoke up. Saying, "I have a free day today, but tomorrow going to be back at work." "I would like to organize for you all to come over and see where I'm working." "Would you like to do this as a family?"

"Oh yes," "dad we would like to see your place of work," Amanda Denise and oneself said so. You need at least a day to be acclimatized to the weather as it is scorching in the day. So you must all make sure that you are wearing your sunscreen, I would not want you to get burnt on the 1st day. Is there anything that you would all like to do together today? The girl said we would love to see the shops and go into town. Dad said that was an excellent idea and a good way for you to get your bearings. Therefore, this is what we will do; we should all go out to town, and one will show you the best and easiest route to walk into town. As it's not far,

What do you think of this then son? Excellent dad, it will be fun. That has settled then a unanimous decision. Amanda and Denise looked at each other; one could pretty much understand what their thoughts were. Shopping! As they smiled at one another. One thought to oneself just another chance to explore. Dad took one sip from his coffee cup, and then started to eat his cooked breakfast. We will follow father's lead. We did not need much encouragement as the breakfast looked delicious. Suddenly the houseboy left the room. Denise said it looked like we have a little visitor. Who could this be one thought? Our little furry friend Suttee has appeared in the room as if by magic at the same time scaring the houseboy away. Suttee found a small spot on the floor in front of the window. Anywhere the sun was blazing through the coke wooden louvered blinds. He rolled on the floor as if he was scratching his back, kicking his legs in the air at the same time as playful cats do. Then Suttee started to walk around in small circles, and then curled up on the floor. He looks so cute and fluffy. Dad finished his breakfast and put his knives and forks together on his plate, and then he began to read his paper. Browsing through and over the interesting headlines of his paper. The Zambian times he called it. Father pondered over the front page for a while. You could watch him smile, from within his personality. "There it is in black-and-white," father said unexpectedly. "It is now officially in print." What is it farther we all asked together? Then we all looked at each other waiting for an answer. Dad says; Colin has put the information in the press about the new directorship. That has made all of us very pleased as now it is entirely official, in the Zambian times. One placed their knife and fork together on the plate followed quickly by one's two sisters.

Dad folded up the paper and then placed it on the corner of the table. We all had a moment; you can say that it was a family moment of joy for our father. In the silence, you could tell that our dad was very pleased with the outcome of the news. One raised one's orange juice as if to present a toast Denise, and Amanda followed suit shortly after with dad's coffee cup we all clash these drinks together. Over the table and said cheers altogether. Dad said, for the future of the family we are united. Amanda said, for the future of dad's new business. In addition, we all cheered again. Along sip from our drinks, this sealed the toast. What a happy family we felt this moment. These moments are like gold dust.

Dad said. Think this is dropping us a little hint, of what sort of business father, associated with too. Before words were mentioned similar to this in the Chinese restaurant only the other night. One's father was always known to keep his cards close to his chest.

Dad always tried to teach his broken family the same. Another toast to new beginnings father said. Here here. A chink of glasses with dad's coffee cup, we finished off the contents of our drinking vessels. The family is bonding again; every moment seems so precious with one another. Don't you agree?

45.

Straight from the dining room table into the car. A short journey into the African town center, marketplace.

The journey has taken 5 min in the car.

Father: let us show you all, the shopping center, and then one will show you around the marketplace.

Dad is holding the door open, for us. Therefore, we can walk quickly into the shopping center. What we can all see, Rows upon rows of shelves were quite empty. You could see this is where food products are supposed to be sold. Occasionally they would be one or two items spaced out on the shelves, in the supermarket. There were cases of Fanta, Coca-Cola. Coca-Cola, Fanta, the biggest advertisers. We could see signs everywhere. In addition, we had to have one each. The soft drink companies have a monopoly on the advertising.

Dad: there you go Tom,

Tom Thank you. Dad: one for you Denise. Thank you (with a smile)

Dad: also one for you Amanda. Amanda: "Thank you" (with a smile). Dad: opening each bottle using his bottle of Fanta to open the rest. Popping of all our bottle tops with ease. We were all quite amazed, on how he did this.

Dad: levered one of the tops off. Using a second bottle to use it appropriately as a bottle opener

Tom is thinking: It looked impressive one must add to oneself as the father was opening the bottles. Each drink cost approximately 0.25 engway currency exchange in (British pound sterling this would be the equivalent of about £0.02p a bottle. Sincerely the cost of living in Africa at that time was very reasonable. We have to stay close to our father as we are all still getting used to the environment. There was not much to see in the shops. Nevertheless, dad wanted to show us how little there was in the town for sale. Therefore showing us how privilege we were in the UK

Dad: showed us around the supermarket. The service that are provided by the supermarkets is very sparse, children. It was cooler in the shade of the supermarket shop, escaping from the bright sunlight; it did not seem that there were many people in the supermarket. Except one gentleman, working. Pulling a trolley through the Supermarket Aisles full of the large brown paper parcel, which seemed hefty? Dad: "sugar! Delivery". As the shop, assistant stopped in the Aisles and opened the brown paper parcel. Then began to stack the shelves in front of us, people started to walk all around us as they must have been following the trolley, with the sugar on-board. Every time a man put something on the shelf, people took it off again. Tom: once thinking to one why don't they just take it straight off the trolley?

Therefore, one asked oneself father this. Dad: they have to follow protocol Tom. Tom: ok (with an interested nod of the head) the sugar completely sold in minutes. Dad: right children let us get on with the tour (looking at us all and smiling) and then walked us along the corridor to the main door and out onto the street. Then walked us all together along the Street. On the right-hand side was a large cinema complex, and above it was a restaurant called the captain's cabin. Dad: telling us how much of a fabulous restaurant this is. We all walked together further on down the street. Passing an old African woman, who was selling fruit juices in plastic bags. We did not realize the poverty as we were walking down the street. I suppose that we were not unquestionably accustomed to seeing what poverty looks close. As none of us has ever seen here before. A few nervous glances from a man walking on the opposite side of the road made one's two sisters a little bit uncomfortable. Sure that they felt safe. As we are all within a group. We walked a little further; we could hear a lot of calling. Dad said; we are approaching the marketplace everybody keeps closing together call out if Anyone occur isolated behind. Keep an eye on each other, please. Dad said this in such a way not to panic us, but also to keep us nice and tight in a family group. Well, we all walked around the corner together. In addition, there was a welcome sight. It looked beautiful. All different coloured vegetables, dried meat. All laid out on plastic bags;

everybody was sitting down on the floor. Offering their wares to any passers-by these credible potential customers.

Dad: all the meat is very fresh out here as the meat slaughtered in the morning and sold in the afternoon. Especially around African markets

Tom: notice somebody selling meat. Not a vacuum sealed as in the UK but open to the elements. (Not very hygienic) The meat remains covered with flies; we could smell the fresh blood in the air. This lovely little old lady just waved her hand gently to move them along without much joy. As the insects, just kept flying back we all started to understand why father wanted so much food bringing back, from the UK. There was a man selling tins of baked beans in tomato sauce.

Dad: these tins of baked beans are very expensive besides they are out of date. There were lots of chanting! Calling! Out to us to buy things. There was quite a crowd of people there. When we walked through the market people were very polite and made way for us. One can say that it was an incredible experience walking around the marketplace; one did not see one single white person beside us.

Denise: squealed out in shock. Turned round sharply, there was a young boy holding his hands together, as he was begging for small change.

Dad said to Denise quietly: leave him alone. Let oneself sort this out. He put his hand in his pocket pulling out some coins speaking in a foreign language (Afrikaans) (that it is the native tongue of Africa.) The young boy smiles he seems to be very pleased.

Dad: placed a few coins into the young boy's hand. The young boy looked up with his big brown eyes and spoke a few words of which we deduced as saying

Thank! You, in his native tongue.

Dad: "When you give any money to anybody make sure that you only show him or her what you give him or her." "Do not show them anymore." "Do not give out more than one at a time." "As the word will travel," "and you may get a group of children wanting money from you." "It is not good as it can get out of hand so you must all be very careful." "Especially when you are giving someone a donation Please, remember this child."

We experienced just what dad was bringing to our attention. The day we arrive at the airport Car park. Oneself and one's sister's experienced this comparable Ambivalent incident while loading luggage into the car Sure enough moments later; there were four more children standing by us, within moments.

Dad: "children we have to go." Tom: (thinking) One found this quite upsetting as well as oneness sisters. As some, children are dressed in rags, dirty clothes.

Tom: slid his hand into his pocket, pulling out a 5K note, which is the equivalent of one-month wages, so we later found out.

Dad: seen oneself handing it out. Amanda Denise: sisters did the same. The children were squealing with excitement you could tell all this from the smiles on their faces. They could not believe it.

They ran off Animated.

Dad: (assertively) it's time for us to leave right now. We made our way back to the car. We could hear shouting screaming behind us. What's going on? All of us turning about quickly and seeing Police: officer-grabbing hold of the child. Attempting and succeeding in taking the money off the African boy.

Police, Immediately bringing the child back to us with the money, after he noticed that we had all saw him. Policemen: was not gentle with the young African boy. He tried to accuse this child of stealing from us. Father: spoke to the Policeman was explaining everything in his native tongue.

Policeman: put out his hand also begging for some money.

Dad: he pulled out a fistful of change from his pocket.

Gave it to the police officer. The police officer only then decided to let go of the Young African Child. Nevertheless, this greedy policeman still kept hold of the 5k notes. Also the change, slipping the note in his pocket along with the coins. Dad: children let's go right now. This corrupt police officer has taken the money from one's father also off this young, poor boy dressed in rags. Family: This moment was very upsetting. However, a stark reminder of what truly goes on. Only because mankind received a police uniform does this give him the right to steal the money?

Apparently so. Dad: said. (corruption in society is this not familiar)

46. Let's move on quietly. We made our way through the crowd. Out of the marketplace to a small shop.

Dad spoke to a shopkeeper in Afrikaans; the shopkeeper pointed towards the back of the shop. Then dad said: children this way. We all walked through the shop, out of the back door to where the car stood parked.

Father: had used the shopkeepers shop to get us out of trouble, away from the marketplace from that horrible policeman. The car park seemed quite quiet.

Dad: well that was quite eventful.

Denise: the boy's dad

Dad: "oh yes look there they are, they have managed to buy some drinks (Coca-Cola Fanta.)" One of the young boys had a pineapple in his hand he was walking towards us confidently. A few moments later, they were right by us. 2 of the boys stood back. The youngest boy out of the 4 Children with a pineapple. Walking towards oneself, holding up a luscious pineapple, offered it to me as a fundamental gift.

47. Young boy speaks out with a smile: Sancho McQuarrie,

Dad: this is Afrikaans he is saying thank you very much. Go on! Tom you can accept this gift

Tom thank you (with a smile)

African boy: smiled back >> Tom: taking the pineapple with gratitude off the young boy with a heartfelt feeling. As this young boy have given more than he has received from the fault of the police officer. This young African boy was the young Virtuous boy that lost his 5K note to the policeman.

Tom: wanted to give some more money to the younger African boy.

But that just would not be right. This sentimental gift of a pineapple it was just amazing. The connection that this young African boy had made with me was incredible. As it brought back memories of my school days drawing the still life in the classroom with my art teacher. Only a month ago and now I'm standing in a foreign country with the juiciest pineapple I have ever seen in my hands. Words cannot express this moment. I have done my best to present this beautiful moment to you. Can we ever make a difference?

Dad: in the car children let go!

Amanda: "what a lovely young boy" as she sat in the front seat. Denise and I stepped into the car and sat down in the back seat, closing the doors, looking out of the windows and the young boys. Standing there in a row with their soft drinks in their hands with big smiles as if it was Christmas day.

Amanda: "We made a difference we made somebody happy."

Tom: I felt the tears well up inside as Dan started to drive away. Denise waved at the young boys through the back window of the car, Tom looked over towards his sister and said quietly do you want to make a difference. Are you thinking about the same thing that I'm thinking Denise said yes instantly with fondled around in our pockets looking for any spare money we have? Denise dad can we Open windows please, father obliged and said yes you May. As soon as the Windows were down Denise and Tom emptied their pockets of all the money that they had out of the window right at the feet of the young boys. The notes were curling in the air as they fell to the ground as the car passed the boys. As their dad steadily drove away. We felt an overwhelming accomplishment of making these four young boys very rich. Denise and I hope that they all managed to use this money wisely and keep it away from that corrupted police officer.

48

Head in the direction of home.

Dad: "that special pineapple looks delicious son," "do you know how to tell if it is ripe enough to eat."

Tom: "know I don't dad."

Dad: "just grab hold of one of the leaves on the top and give it a tug,"

Tom: gently picks at one of the leaves (poking out of the top of the fruit), (giving it a little tug) 1 of the leaves popped out easily.

Dad: "if it is difficult to pull the leaves out. Then the pineapple is not ready to eat. Did you know that before son."

Tom: "know I did not know this we have never seen one of these before dad. Just heard about them at school."

Dad: "These are little tricks of the trade, when we get back home to the bungalow, and I will get the house boy to show you how to cut a pineapple up. He is very skilled at this."

Tom: "one will look forward to this." Having got this delicious looking prickly pineapple on one's lap. Denise: leaned across the seat and grabbed hold of one of the spiky thick waxy leaves to try this for herself. It quickly with ease came away in her hand.

Tom: smiled knowing full well that this fruit, pineapple is ripe. All of us are going to have a treat.

Denise: said, "an interesting texture to the leaf,"" thick and waxy."

Tom: handed the whole pineapple over to Denise. Denise took it in her hands gingerly. Using great caution as Denise did not know how prickly that fruit was. As it was the 1st time my sister had ever seen, Or even held one of these before.

Denise: said, "Oh this is prickly before we know it." Denise was holding the pineapple under her arm like a baby and making cooing noises. As if she was nursing a small child to sleep.

Tom: said, "that's going to be one hell of an ugly! Baby" Denise smiled back in a delightful manner, pretending to be motherly to this pineapple. One just have to sit there watching her as she played with this delicious pineapple as if it was a small baby. It was hilarious and grabbed the whole attention of the car at the time.

Dad piped up and said "you should not play with your food," and laughed out loud. Everyone in the car howled out in laughter!

Tom: this, brings beautiful memories into the family. (family bonding.) Relaxed atmosphere, which everybody can enjoy. The short animated journey in the automobile seems to take only a moment since we had so much fun! Aforementioned Happened to us over a simple fruit pineapple.

A few moments later, we are all arriving at the bungalow. The usual thing the security guard appears from nowhere and opens the gates with a little acknowledgement from the security guard in the way of a salute to our dad. The car drove smoothly into the car park area underneath the car Port.

Dad opens the door of the car first, and we all followed abandoning the vehicle One by one walking into the bungalow.

Dad called out, and he says: —houseboy, the houseboy appeared from outside the bungalow walking straight into the kitchen and bowed graciously to my father.

Dad said, please may you prepare my son's pineapple for the family.

Yes, bowaner, says the houseboy.

Dad says; also a pot of tea for the family, please.

Yes bowaner says the houseboy instantly the houseboy would get to his task after washing his hands in the kitchen sink.

The family retired to the living room finding a nice comfortable chair to sit on in front of the fireplace.

Tom takes his shoes and socks off crushing his toes and feet into the lion skin rug Tom Said. Oh, that feels so nice!

Dad said, "this lion died of old age, Safari Park. Is not poached."

Denise said, "poached?" And giggled,

Amanda said, "what you meant the lion skin is not an egg."

Immediately, dad said no! I mean here he was not shot by criminals. Here is what you mean by poaching; Denise said."

Dad said, yes there is a lot of poaching in Africa it is causing a major problem with the safari parks and reserves.

Tom pulled back his toes off the line skin rug as if he felt a little bit disturbed of putting his feet on a dead animal.

Dad noticed this and said, no need to worry Tom; this animal lived a very happy life on reserves and once again he said that the lion died of old age.

Tom felt a little bit more accustomed to this. I wanted to feel the soft furry skin once again. And pushed his feet further into the rug. Thick, deep Golden colours of the fur skin. Flickering between his toes as he felt the wild animals fur while he was syncing his feet deep into the animals hide, oh feel so good thinking about himself.

Moments later, the cat jumped out of the fireplace. And startled everybody in the room. Amanda squeaked as she was stunting a scream. (Placing her hand over her mouth in shock, to prevent an embarrassing moment. From little fluffy kitty cat) Little Sutty was up to his tricks again. He was purring and walking around the tail end of the lion skin rug,

Dad said Sutty simply does not like to stare into the big cat's eyes. That moment large double doors open into the room a few seconds later; the houseboy walks into the room. With a tray filled with china cups and saucers. Also, a large pot of tea. The houseboy graciously quietly enters the living room area, walks up to the side table next to my dad's chair places the tray down on a small table in the room. Then proceeds to serve my father's Tee. Placing the sugar lumps into his tea with silver tongues. Then proceeded to the next, Denise was next. The houseboy did the same again but asked in a gesture How much sugar that she would like. By holding the bowl of sugar lumps in front of Denise. And holding the sugar tongs on a small silver tray offering Denise service of sugar in one cup of tea.

Denise said; no sugar for me thank you. The houseboy placed the little silver tray containing the sugar bowl and the silver tongues back on The main large tray. Then the houseboy offered her milk in another small silver jug. Denise nodded yes please she said. The houseboy poured a small amount of milk into that piping hot tea. Once he's had it; he's finished. He moved to the next sister Amanda.

Amanda said this was very nice thank you very much I will have two sugars and milk, please. The houseboy served Amanda with exquisite manners. Then the houseboy moved graciously to where Tom was also sitting offering him also a cup of tea. Pouring it gently from the teapot, without making a single noise.

Tom said two sugars and milk please. The houseboy served. Then collected the tray and carried the tray away. Walking, straight out of the room through the double doors. Placing the tray out of sight down on the table, outside the room.

Turning round returning promptly back into the room with another tray with the gorgeous pineapple on it. Also bowls with a jug of fresh cream to pour over fresh juicy, delicious pineapple. The houseboy placed a tray containing the pineapple on the little table beside my father's chair. The houseboy grabs hold of what remained left of the leaves on the top of the pineapple and lifted the pineapple up. Wow! The skin came away from the pineapple fruit. Leaving the juicy Gold Yellow pile of pineapple rings on the plate. The houseboy then placed the empty skin next to the stack of pineapple rings. We all applauded him as if he was a magician. You could see that he was pleased with his accomplishment, but the houseboy kept his composure.

The houseboy served each member of the family in the room starting with the father and then the girls and then myself.

The service was impeccable and the food delicious. The houseboy walked graciously out of the room holding the tray again. Repeating the way he did it before with a tea tray, but this time he walked back into the room and upright stood by the doors looking towards, My dad.

With his hands clasped together in front of his self. And slightly bowed his head. One's dad said yes. That will be all, thank you very much. The houseboy then walked backwards out of the room holding the double door handles and closing them gently and quietly as he left the room accompanied with a low bow from the waist.

Dad said, "right children, on the agenda, tasting this delicious pineapple so what do you think of it well."

The room beamed with smiles, and everybody pretty much together said "delicious" with a smile as we are all trying this juicy, delicious tropical fruit.

Tom's thinking, this is the most delicious thing that I have ever tasted in my life so sweet and juicy. And I'm sure that everybody at a specially my two sisters was thinking the same. As it showed in their expressions on their faces.

Dad mentioned "well children do you

Think you are going to come into Africa and just see a small town. I have arranged for us to travel to Victoria Falls and Zimbabwe."

The silence in the room with emotion was intense but brimming with excitement as the children looked at each other and then turned to look at their father.

Dad smiled back. "So we are going to explore Africa together what do you think of this their children?"

Tom said, "exploring love it."

Denise is very pleased as she had already been working on a project from school something to do with Victoria Falls.

Denise says proudly "As it happens to be the largest curtain of water in the world."

Dad immediately responds and says, "yes. Victoria Falls presents a spectacular sight of awe-inspiring beauty and grandeur on the Zambezi River, forming the border between Rhodesia and Zimbabwe. That Described by the Kololo tribe living in the area in the 1800's as 'Mosi-Oa-Tunya' – 'The Smoke that Thunders'. In more modern terms, Victoria Falls is known as the greatest curtain of falling water in the world.

Columns of spray can be seen from miles away. In the height of the rainy season, More than five hundred million cubic meters of water per minute plummet over the edge. Over a width of nearly two kilometers, into a gorge over one hundred meters below. The wide, basalt cliff over which the falls thunder, transforms the Zambezi from a placid river into a ferocious torrent cutting through a series of dramatic gorges. Facing the Falls is another sheer wall of basalt, rising to the same height, and capped by mist-soaked rain forest. A path along the edge of the forest provides the visitor prepared to brave the tremendous spray, with an unparalleled series of views of the Falls. One special vantage point is across the Knife edge Bridge. Where visitors can have the finest view of the Eastern Cataract and the Main Falls as well as the Boiling Pot, where the river turns and heads down the Batoka Gorge. Other vantage points include the Falls Bridge, Devils Pool and the Lookout Tree, both of which command panoramic views across the Main Falls. So what do you think of this than children?"

"Wonderful Dad."

we all agreed (smiling with excitement the thought of adventure.)

Amanda said, "when are we leaving."

"Tomorrow morning!"

Tom looks over to Denise and smiles. Denise smiled back and then we both looked over and listened attentively to what dad was saying.

"It is going to be a long journey and it will take a few days for us to get there. So we must prepare ourselves for a long journey. We have a few places to stop off at, and it is going to be a holiday inside a holiday. I also have a little bit of work to carry out. As your father, we are all on a journey. But this will not interrupt our holiday too much. We will stop over near various hotels to see as much as the countryside at close hand as we possibly can. Who knows! What this adventure is going to present to us."

A buzz of excitement filled the room.

Dad pulled out a map. Unfolding it, at the same time as he was laying it down on the floor. Right next to the Lions' head.

And proceeded to point at the place where we are on the map then with his other hand he explains to us how far we had to travel. "Approximately 2500 miles there. Travelling across open countryside as a family. It is the only way to see Africa."

Father said, "we might even go on a little safari. So this evening we need to pack a few clothes and make sure that all the checks stand completed on the vehicle. Tom you can give me a hand with this."

"Yes!" "I will love to Dad,"

Dad Aske's, "Are there any questions from anyone?

Amanda asking, "What time will be leaving in the morning?"

Dad "We'll leave as soon as the sun rises. So it is bed early tonight for all of us. But 1st of all? We are going out to the rugby club as I want you to meet the team. And the club members. Or, on the other hand, would you like to go to the pictures. Or the theatre?"

(Dad smiles as he pulls out a handful of tickets from down the side of his chair. Displaying four lovely Tickets for the

Theatre club. Fanning them out in his fingers displaying the tickets in all their glory.)

"Oh, what are we going to watch?..... Oliver Twist."

Amanda says "yes.!" EXCITEDLY Pretty much the same time

Denise also speaks out and says "the theatre."

Tom also agrees on the theatre. Experience, as mentioned above, is going to be great fun! We always have fun at the theatre.

Dad says, "right children we have about 2 hours to get ready.

Tom, "cum with me now, and we will check the car out. Girls, get your clothes packed something for the evening something to wear in the car, and make sure you have all your sun creams with you."

The houseboy is in the kitchen he is already preparing refreshments for the journey.

Tom jumps up pulling his socks and shoes on. Getting ready now to go out and help his father with a car.

Dad stands up out of his comfortable armchair; the girls are already moving out of the room to start packing. In one little suitcase.

"Come on son, Let's get going."

Out of the bungalow walking underneath the car Port, dad has managed to lift the bonnet; showing Tom, where are all the important parts to check in the car.

to prepare it for a long journey.

"I've already done the major services. At the garage the day before. So we do not have too much to do Tom, but I will show you what needs doing before going on, any long trip as this is a serious test for the car. Even a small problem such as a worn windscreen wiper, or an out-of-balance tire can produce troubles on the journey."

Dad is saying a few important, but simple preventative measures to prepare your vehicle for a long trip. A checklist such as brakes and suspension these components are important, so this may only be inspected by a mechanic in a garage with a hydraulic car ramp. My usual mechanic has completed the main maintenance components with an oil change, tire balancing and mechanical inspection. Don't leave it until the last moment Tom, do this a few days before your long journey, and you will never have any problems. Touch wood son." (dad makes a fist, with a flick of his wrist. 'Knock!' 'Knock!' saying, "On Wood," hitting the wooden post.

('a deep sound Bump' 'Bump.')

(Dad placed his hand on his head for a moment and smiled. Then brushed his hair away from his eyes)

Then saying, "perfect preparation prevents a poor performance all the P's son. Remember this one? Say this every time you are going to do something important Perfect preparation prevents a p**s poor performance don't use this swear word in front of the girls. As you must be a gentleman." Tom, "Okay, dad, let's be realistic. I will keep this to myself I promise you Dad,

"Also what are the rest of the checks?" Tom says hey! "Check the owner's manual for details."

- Under the hood;
- Engine oil;
- Transmission fluid;
- Engine coolant;
- Battery;
- Air filter;
- Lights and mirrors;
- Windshield wipers;
- Tires;
- Steering, suspension and drivetrain; components;
- Spare tire, wheel wrench and the jack;
- Basic emergency kit, above all, make sure; you have a map Tom and plenty of water;

End of the Show at the Theatre Club

In the theatre filled with exciting emotions of the show. With a standing ovation after the family as just experienced a live performance of Oliver Twist, walking out of the dimly lit theatre, negotiating the steps lit by a torch by a theatre assistant. Filled with emotions and excitement of the drama.

Denise looked at me and said "did you enjoy that Tom" while we were walking. And holding out her hand to help me negotiate the crowd so that we would stay together. Down the steps, and into the foyer a garden. There was a raised border filled with flowers and a perfect lawn scattered with a few picnic tables bringing the outside in, as they say.

The 1st door on the left for the toilets next to that was the exit doors. And next to the exit doors was the doors for the bar. As I was not old enough to go with them into the pub we all waited outside, the father then said, "wait here I will get you some drinks." And promptly father disappeared. A young lady spoke to us. "Whom dad was talking to just a moment ago. My name is Claudia she said.

With a sweet angel voice and a lovely smile. (Tall with rich blonde hair and blue eyes a beautiful smile). Tom was instantly mesmerised by the beautiful woman.

Claudia said, "did you all enjoy the show?"

Tom said "oh yes,"

Denise said, "yes, but where is Amanda."

Tom "She has walked to the bar with dad."

Amanda is the only one that is old enough out of the children to go to the bar. Presenting father, helpful assistance with the round of drinks.

Claudia says, "Oliver Twist remains played by all of the local children; none of them are professional actors, but they all do it so well. I understand that you have just landed the other day in Africa. We have all been waiting to see Jim's children. And what lovely children you are."

Denise says; "it's nice to meet you cloudier! Do you have children yourself."

Cloudier. "No, I'm afraid not, Denise. I am young and not yet married." (With a smile)

in Just a moment,

Dad turned up with Amanda, carrying the drinks.

Dad and Amanda handed out the drinks also to Claudia.

The conversation blossomed all about Oliver Twist;

And These young actors. The foyer stayed crowded with people All around us.

Tom was mesmerised with the beautiful Claudia. All 3 of our children instantly made an excellent connection with Claudia. You could see that she knows how to connect with children.

Dad mentioned that we were heading off tomorrow on an adventure to Victoria Falls.

Claudia says, "that is going to be a trip of a lifetime you all so much going to enjoy the beautiful experiences of Victoria Falls."

Dad smiles back.

Amanda finally speaks! And ask the question. To cloudier. "Have you ever been to Victoria Falls before."

Claudia Answering, "Oh yes, I have also stayed in the hotel Called the Victoria Falls. With a large swimming pool and fantastic nightlife and entertainment. The Ideal spot for the whole family. I'm sure you are all going to have a wonderful time."

Claudia takes a dainty sip from the glass.

Amanda asked straight out with this with no warning whatsoever.

"You dad's girlfriend!" she says,

Claudia immediately looked up with those big blue eyes and an embarrassing smile.

"I don't know how to answer that. because as I'm sure at the moment your father is not truly in a relationship with anyone, I presume."

Dad quickly changes the subject to save an embarrassing moment for Claudia. After looking at Amanda and shaking his head.

And then looking at cloudier smiling with a hint of embarrassment.

Dad says, "children would you like to know what cloudier does. She is a sports trainer she helped with the training of the rugby team."

Buzz Of light-hearted conversation to break the ice. From

Amanda's idiotic notions and rudeness. But deep down truthfully, I know that Amanda was not the only one thinking about this. As I too was wishing that Claudia was dad's girlfriend. A little hint of sadness but also a hint of joy. It is so hard to tell. But knowing full well that we would like to see a lot more of cloudier. As she is an absolute dream personality to talk too.

Tom put out his hand to Claudia. Claudia bent down slightly and felt Tom's hand.

Tom said, "you could be our friend innocently."

Claudia smiled and said: –"Oh yes most definitely!" Appropriately Dad said, "cloudier you are excepted into the family now!" (Happy Smiles) from everyone.

Tom said, "which school did you go to Claudia."

Claudia, "why Tom, so nice of you to ask. I went to an all girls school called 'Roedeing,' You will find it situated in Brighton in the UK."

Dad says, "this happens to be one of the finest finishing schools for ladies. Claudia is a debutante."

Tom replies, "Impressive."

Claudia smiles once again. Her brilliant white teeth and her gorgeous personality were just flowing through.

Tom says, "Claudia what is a debutante?"

Cloudier says, "an upper-class young woman making her first appearance in fashionable society."

Denise, "please tell us more about this Claudia."

Claudia "yes, of course, Denise. A debutante or deb (from the French débutante, female beginner). is a girl or young lady. From an aristocratic or upper class family who has reached the age of maturity and, as a new adult, are then introduced to society at a formal debut presentation. Originally, it meant the young woman was eligible to marry, and part of the purpose was to display her to eligible bachelors and their families with a view to marriage within a select upper class circle.

A distinguished committee may recommend debutantes or sponsor by an established member of elite society.

Debut presentations vary by regional culture and are also frequently referenced as debutante balls, cotillion balls or, coming-out-parties! The male equivalent does often referred to as beautician ball. Alone debutante might have her debut, or she might share it with a sister or other close relative. Modern debutante balls are often charity events: the parents of the debutante donate a certain amount of money to a designated cause, and the guests pay for their tickets. These balls may be elaborate formal affairs and involve not only (deb's) but junior debutantes, escorts and ushers, flower girls and pages as well."

Denise, "Wow! Seems so exciting."

All of us are mesmerised by Claudia's beauty and education. Somebody for the 1ˢᵗ time and having such an impact, as my father always says 1ˢᵗ impressions count. And you can say Claudia has made an excellent 1ˢᵗ impression. With duty and charisma." Claudia as beauty far surpasses any female that I have ever seen.

50

Claudia personality was riveting;

Tom and Denise looked at each other and came up to the same conclusion you want to see Claudia and more often.

Denise said to Tom, "are you thinking the same thing that I'm thinking." While Denise looked up at Claudia and glanced back down to Tom again, (creating communication eye to eye contact with each other.) "Oh yes,"

Denise Tom said together quietly with excitement. The thoughtful expression from Denise was all it took.

Denise said innocently to dad. "Dad! can Claudia come to Victoria Falls with us, please."

Dad says, "Oh no Denise cloudy is far too busy for that she is working with the rugby club. But it's a very nice thought and if we had had a little bit more time we may have been able to arrange something."

Claudia says, "yes that is correct I do have a full diary this week. But I am triumphal that you have offered an invitation to me Denise."

Tom said, "this would be so nice for you to be a guest of the family. We could have gone swimming in the pool, and you could have looked after us while dad was working."

Denise says, "it would have been so perfectly beautiful."

(while she was smiling at Tom.) You could seriously say that Claudia was an instant hit with all of the children.

Dad says, "I tell you what. If Claudia doesn't mind, we can arrange something later on after we have come back from our exploring holiday."

Claudia Says, "one would enjoy spending time with your children Jim."

So this will have to be arranged if cloudier agrees with Jim. Over a handshake is if a business transaction has just taken place.

Denise and Tom stared at each other with a smile of expression and teamwork acknowledgement.

Dad says "come on children let's say goodbye to cloudy, as we have an early start in the morning; we need to get some rest."

Denise gave cloudier a little smile and said "it is a pleasure meeting you cloudier;"

Claudia leaned down and spoke to all of the children "it is very nice to meet you. You do have lovely children Jim."

Tom just could not resist his self and step forward and gave Claudia a Cuddle. (Tom could feel Claudius warm firm but soft body in his arms Tom just did not want to let go of Claudia) Claudia responded and put her arms out to all of the children and gave us all a group cuddle. Oh, this was so helpful and friendly for all of us.

Dad said come on kids that's enough for this evening we have to go. Buy, buy, Claudia. We all said goodbye.

Dad gave cloudier a long handshake. The children looked intensively as their eyes were locked together we are just hoping dad will make a pass at Claudia. But this did not take place at this moment. And the opportunity passed as We all turned round and left while cloudier was waving.

Claudia was saying "by children have a safe journey and take care Jim, see you all when you get back from your holiday." As we are walking out of a large glass double doors out and away from the theatre club.

The short journey back home to the bungalow informed with the conversation of Claudia and how much we truly like her.

Dad agreed with us on how gorgeous and fascinating idea was. Father agreed that we would be able to see her again. Tom was thinking; he cannot wait to see the lovely Claudia again. And I'm sure that the girls were thinking the same as him as well as their Dad. After the holiday break.

Denise says, "that she is so beautiful."

"Agreed" Tom.

These few moments with a real pleasant personality took effect on the children. I do believe our Father all so was very intrigued in the beautifully educated and remarkably impressive young lady. The whole journey back to the bungalow just seemed like a dream after meeting Claudia.

Into the bungalow waiting in the kitchen for a nice hot drink before, we go to bed

dad always makes a gorgeous hot chocolate drink before bedtime.

It gives the family time to unwind and reflect on the experiences of the day. Also, thoughtfully preparing for the next morning exciting adventures. Are soon to begin

Adventures

In the ghostly hours of the early morning. Hearing rustling noise at Tom's bedroom door,

What is it?

Suddenly in the pitch black house. The door opened slowly a tall shadow appeared in the doorway.

Tom felt a fear come over his body, as he was half asleep and not fully aware of his surroundings.

Is it the vampire thing?

Is it somebody to get me?

We wonder what went through Tom's mind?

Still half in a dream sleep and half awake.

The fear intensified as the dark silhouetted person proceeded closer to the bed.

Tom could feel his body tensing up with fear as if he was protecting his self from a terrible thing that is going to happen. Then suddenly the tense moment unravel itself as a dark silhouette came extremely close to Tom's face. Tom was beginning to squirm in bed with fear; in need to squeeze his eyes tightly shut just wishing that this horrible thing would go away. He could feel the warm moist breath of the shadow next to his cheek. Tom thinks of holding his breath to avoid the smell of the evil sulphur breath, and instantly thinking is this Peter.

Oh, no, no, Oh no! (Panic starting to intensify inside Tom's mind.)

And then the breath whispered to Tom. "Tom Good morning son, it's time to get up." (smelling of fresh mint toothpaste not sulphur halitosis breath this time. as these thoughts have been programmed into Tom's subconscious mind from his stepfather over time.)

"Get some breakfast in the kitchen. Good morning, my son."

The tension of Tom's body at that moment totally relaxed.

Tom exhales the stressful pressure as he had been holding his breath. At this point, Tom opened his eyes. The "Good --- morning -- dad," Tom spoke quietly to his father.

"Wake up son it's time to get up and get dressed." "The adventure starts now!" "Meet the family in the kitchen for breakfast."

Dad then disappeared through the doorway and closed the door behind him.

Tom could hear the footsteps disappearing down the hallway as the steps became further away. Apparently, Dad was waking up the girls next. Tom thought to himself. That was so close I am in a safe place now Peter Could not touch me he is at home in the UK. 148 hours (6,832.7 miles away from me) if he drove. At this moment, Tom sprang out of bed, rushing to get his clothes on that had been already laid out as Tom had done this the night before while he was packing a bag. Moments later, Tom was speeding into the kitchen. A display of breakfast cereal boxes. The smell of cooking bacon, eggs, the aroma was filling the kitchen cooked by the houseboy. Moments later dad walked into the kitchen "good morning Tom" father said.

Tom along with a little teardrop in his eye lunges forward giving dad a big hug around the waist.

Dad said, "good morning what do I owe for this pleasure."

"You are my dad, and I love you Dad," Tom said sweetly to his father.

"I love you to son so very much" while speaking to Tom picking him up and placing his young son Tom on the chair next to the breakfast table With a caring fatherly smile, Dad said Tom, "Come on let's get some breakfast together."

At that moment, the girls walk into the kitchen.

"Good morning father," the girls said together "good morning Tom."

Dad "Just-in-time girls, the houseboy, is dishing up breakfast what perfect timing girls." Dad said, "so Everyone who matters has joined the breakfast table."

Tom's thinking to himself, It seems unusual. That the mother is not here with us, Tom did not mention this at breakfast, but I'm sure it was on the girl's mind as well as toms. What is, mom up to in the UK and why is she not here with us it just seems wrong.

Dad said, "a slice of bacon Tom."

Tom replies "yes, please!"

And the dad served the girls as well as Tom bacon and eggs.

Do you know that was the most delicious enjoyable breakfast that anybody could have asked for, Swilled down with tropical fruit juices, with this lovely family company?

all talking about this journey of exciting adventures that awaits us just a few moments away.

The girls are so excited they are talking about the road trip.

Amanda and Denise are saying we can't wait to get going. As the sun was inaugurating on appearance, you could see the room began to light up slightly, the warmth of everybody's smiles of excitement emanates around the kitchen table. Father pours himself a large cup of coffee while pondering over the newspaper. He was checking within the political news Paper to see if there is any trouble spots. Road-blocks checkpoints, etc.

Amanda says, "anything, unusual in the newspaper?"

"In that location is an escaped killer, regarded the police to be extremely dangerous furthermore volatile. Remains at large after he mysteriously got out while being transported from Pollsmoor maximum-security Prison while going to court."

Denise says "that is a shocking story father will we be safe,"

"Oh yes, children for one you are with me and I won't let anything happen to you. Nevertheless that prison is in South Africa, and it is miles away. Everyone is good so no worries there."

(while Dad was, subliminally Biting his lip nervously for a long 2nd) Father says, "we can go. I'm just catching up on the news before we head off."

Tom is taking a final bite of his bacon and egg toasted sandwich. As the sun beams through the window father squinted a little bit as the sun streamed into his eyes and the early morning sunrise takes effect. "Okay, children" father says "has everybody finished.

Tom is still eating his last bit of breakfast. The houseboy walks past us all with a suitcase. As the family are still sitting down at the table. Presumably he was placing them in the car.

Dad pulls out an imaginary checklist out of his pocket as a bit of a joke. Looking at the empty palm of his hand saying, "checklist! Three children and one adult, suitcases and refreshments. Patting the top of his flask on the top of the lid. Flask check" he says. "We won't get far without my cup of coffee," dad says.

Tom acutely says, "chequebook." (everybody laughed). While making their way to the car, Tom jumps off his chair along with Denise and Amanda.

Dad takes one last mouthful of his coffee swallows it and then says "The adventure begins. Road trip! Anyone? Anyone for a road trip."

"The three children shout out yes 'Road trip!" (followed by happy smile from the three children) One by one we all followed father out to the car.

The motorcar was gleaming, freshly cleaned it looked as if it was brand-new if not better.

Amanda is controlling for the front seat again "shouting I'm shotgun!"

Father nodded; Denise ducked into the back seat along with Tom. Father gave the houseboy a brown paper envelope.

The houseboy thanks, dad by bowing showing his appreciation hands together and smiled.

Whatever it was he was extremely appreciated of this. Next Dad jumps into the driver's seat. A clever turn of the key and the engine burst into life. Low revs of the engine then into gear the car rolled backwards slightly. Looking out of the rear window I could see the guard opening the gates.

Dad turned and drove forward driving one lap around the back garden round the bungalow then straight towards the gates and stopped for a moment. As the guard came back into the gates making sure that the road was clear waving our father through the gates. The car drove steadily down to The main road turning left and accelerating away with smooth precision.

"We are off and running." Father cries out.

The children start singing along with dad "we are all going on a summer holiday." everyone in the car Singing at the top of their voices.

The excitement of the road trip and all of its glories of exploration began to unfold. All of the children are looking out through the windows of the car looking at the big posh houses surrounded by massive security walls. You could tell the size of the houses from how many chimneys there were, some houses were very grand indeed. Sometimes you could see through the bars of the gates to see a large house behind. Posh cars Porsches Rolls-Royces Jaguars and other beautiful cars in the drives. Then a left-hand turn, onto a straight piece of road. That went on for about 20 miles this was the outskirts of the town, and you can see many shantytowns minuscule huts with wriggly tin roofs the walls stood made out of mud and straw. Everything there just looks so grimy. Even the children are playing in the streets with no shoes upon their feet. They looked so hot and dusty. It implied poverty, before-mentioned a shame to see human beings like this. That was nothing that we could do that we were utterly powerless all I can think of right now is just to bring it to your attention and help To be your eyes through this book. Whatever way I can, and whatever way you can help.

("you can contact Bill Gates as he has a charity website http:// malarianomore.org.uk/ Please contact our Fundraising Manager, Helen Mabberley, on 020 7801 3840 or email fundraising@malarianomore.org.uk")

Father was travelling at about 60 KPH (37.28MPH) an hour. And then began to accelerate to 120 KPH (74.57MPH) an hour.

Now we are moving. The route was an entirely straight strip of black tarmac running through the bush one could say. The tarmac shimmered supporting the early morning sunlight you could experience the warmth of the sun distorting the vision of the landscape. As the Earth warmed up.

Dad explained this is a mirage image comprised and produced under specific meteorological contingencies, in whichever circumstances relate to being reflected or relocated either in whichever imaginary somethings resemble upon a surface. As an example. Incredible varieties visible patterns during single index of refraction among a base layer of boiling air.

Along with a higher parallel of cold air, Meteorological temperatures can cause visible light rays to curve symbolising a reflective surface distortion incorporating a distorted view. Reflecting underneath objects.

(comprising of the sky, clouds, land based objects). Moving into the ever warmer air. Can be refracted back up again. Children you can truly see an excellent viewing of the individual light rays here. Observe them coming up from the ground and tarmac; can you see a mirror image forming above it. of the scenery and objects, which seem to be lower than the scenery truthfully is.

The sky itself, usually, appears manifested. Appearing in the heat haze generating a reflective surface mirage of a distant lake. While the sun became stronger through the day so did the Mirage effect.

"Dad you are incredible Tom says. Dad?"

Tom speaks out again. "If you cover a car in a heated Metal Skin, you could make it perform to Blend into the Scenery." (By Generating Its Own Mirage Tom Thought To His Self) Dad said, "it seemed so Son, I Never Thought of It in That Way before sun. You Are a Genius Young Man," Father Said.

at That Point, We all settle down in the car for a long journey ahead of us while admiring the beautiful apparitions animations and shapes that the Mirage was causing.

Denise said, "it were just like going to the pictures with popcorn."

Dad pulled out a bag of boiled sweets gave them to Amanda to pass them around the car. These sweets were delicious.

Suddenly in father's rearview mirror he has seen a police car with blue flashing lights driving fast. Within moments, everything changed. Www-Woosh. Fathers car shook slightly. As the police car came speeding past us at such a critical extreme high speeds approximately at (193.12 KPH)120 miles an hour extraordinary speed the police car was at incredibly Dangerously High-Speed at full tilt.

(flat out) Here was the 1st Zambian police car that I have ever seen. It looked out-of-control as this car passed us at this Dangerous extreme speed.

Dad's car was enveloped in a dust cloud from the police car while it flew by us.

Father had to slow down somewhat To Have Chance for The Road to clear ahead to get his visibility back. "For all there must be an emergency or a policeman, is late for his tea." Jokingly.

(Chuckling) Dad remarked. More of the same scenery then Actively abruptly dads car Sharply veered Unexpectedly avoiding Something Dangerous in the Road.

Dad shouts out a pothole!

Denise and I could see out of the back window How big this pothole was. "It was huge" the whole side of the road had collapsed. Amazingly Enough, There remained just enough room for one car, to pass it was lucky that dad was concentrating Clearly on the road to miss it.

"Who knows what May Have occurred if we had of hit it, at such speed!" Answered Dad.

"Oh no, ahead of us there is a car off the road" Tom shouts! out! While he Pointed outside the car window. You could just make out the car in the long grass and see the tracks as the car entered the grass. There was Long launch scratch marks on the tarmac as the car, looked like it had gone out of control. There was no blue flashing light on this car, but it was the police car. You could see the police car markings Clearly on it. There was a horrible looking man standing at the side of the road. Holding a significant stake in his hand using it as a walking stick.

Dad pulled over to the opposite side of the road but did not stop. He carried on regardless. As he drove past a man holding What seemed to be a walking stick. The man raised his stick (or What Looked like a Stick) in the air and started to run towards the car, pointing this stick at us. So that was lucky, huh.

My father used his skilful initiative by turning onto the other side of the road foreseeing the terrible circumstance and moving away from that man. It could be a policeman, or it could be the criminal In the midst of attempting to escape from the prison who want to say. (sending a chilling danger of reality into all of us within the car.) However, we are not going to take unspecified risks.

Dad says, plus he puts his foot down and accelerates away. Obviously the police car had collided with the pothole and rolled knocking off the police lights at the same time. Where there were some dangerous animals in Zambia and not just animals if you get my meaning. Escaped criminals and many other people you may think they are in command. You must always be on look-out for the threat scenario.

Dad says if we had stopped he could have killed all of us and stolen a car. Or even taken us all as a hostage. So never stop you cannot trust these people drive-away ask questions later when you have gone. Is this not the safest way children. I agree yes, we all agreed. The danger is very apparent in Africa. We are all starting to believe that his related to the education and the poverty. One 2nd of kindness without assessing the situation 1st can seriously in danger your health.

Dad said sternly. While still driving away down the road.

Denise looked through the back window and said the man has gone. Must have just disappeared off into the bush dad said. As soon as I find a telephone I will contact my company and let them know where this has happened. He is only an hour out of town. A mysterious, scary silence came over all of us in the car. After driving for approximately 2 hours with no sight of civilisation, suddenly we started to see people walking down the road with large jugs and plastic buckets on their heads. And most of them were female there was one man with them all he was carrying a stick. Only walk in front. We saw them as we drove near.

Dad said, "they were collecting water for their families. And they have a hunter with them to make sure that they are safe." "safe? from what?" Tom then asked. "Safe from Lions Tigers water buffalo, there is lots of Deadly things in the Bush that will attack And kill you."

The people were there one moment and gone the next as we drove past and away along the road. Another 20 or 30 min later the road became very rough, plus there were lots of potholes to negotiate in the road. Soon we came to a small town.

Dad asked if we were all ready for a break yet. Oh yes, dad that would be nice. The roads on the way to the rest stop hotel These Road streets are planted with Bo-Bob trees also palm trees it was very exciting as the buildings look gorgeous. We drove slowly through the town keeping on the same road straight through the town there was a large hotel and dad parked at the car park. "Come with children let's go into this hotel. I will use the phone and Amanda will look after you for a moment while we are in the safety of the hotel foyer reception."

52

Dad said, "Come along children look how beautiful this hotel is."

This Hotel Was Standing alone detached with large paving steps leading up to the grand entrance to the front doors of the hotel. As we all walked up the steps together as a family, the doors were opened for us. Into the great Hotel lobby, we walked into the Hotel entrance, which opened into a divinely decorated hotel foyer. Various seating areas. With the Large counter running the left-hand side of the room. Father walked up to the counter. He asked if he could use the phone. The manager politely presented Father with a telephone.

Dad started to dial at the same time thanking him for the use of the phone. Father began to talk alone. "this is Jim," Dad said. "Can I speak to Lynn, please," after a few moments While the father was HOLDING his hand, over the mouthpiece of the phone. "Children, you can sit down there. Wait for me to finish this call." Without any delay from us, we all sat down in earshot of the telephone conversation. "Hello, Lynn" "Hello, Jim," Lynn said "yes. How can I help you today?"

Jim replies "can you take an urgent memo please Lynn We have come across a little incident on the road driving from our hometown. Which we are all okay. We are about 2 hours away from our destination. But I needed to bring this to your attention for security purposes."

"Lynn said." Yes, go-ahead Jim."

"I do believe that we have seen the man that was described in the newspaper the escaped convict from the prison this morning. He is armed and dangerous with a rifle. The police car has spun off the road afterwards hitting a large pothole at high speed. The family and I are all okay and safe. Can you make sure that the police do immediately informed of this?"

Lynn answers "Yes, Of course, I will do this for you Jim."

"We are going to head on to the next town. I will call you this evening and keep in touch with you for any developments."

Lynn says, "that will be fine Jim." My dad put the phone down safely after saying goodbye to Lynn on the receiver. He turned round to the family and smiles.

Amanda says, "that a rifle then."

Dad says, "I believe so."

"So we were very lucky that time."

We all thought. Knowing full well why the whole family was quite quiet and silent after this shocking experience.

"Okay, children," Father says "so. What would you like to do, would you like to have something to eat here in this hotel. Or would you like to travel a little bit more and stop off at the Hotel that we will be staying at tonight.?"

truthfully we were all thinking about getting as much distance between us as possible from the incident site

That gave us a little question. Aforementioned is between us. What would you do, in that situation? Well,

My tummy was not rumbling at that moment. So I said let's carry on to the next hotel.

Dad agreed on this and also Denise and Amanda. But 1st of all we will go to the bar and have some refreshments I think this is a good idea says the father. It will give us a few minutes to explore this beautiful hotel. An African man appeared in a very nice suit. Also, said would you like me to accompany you to the bar.

Dad agreed with this. And this very smartly dressed gentleman showed us the way through the foyer to a lavishly decorated bar area. Lovely thick carpets and a white grand piano in the room.

"What would you like to drink," Dad asked all 3 of us?

"Fanta Coca-Cola, what would you like Amanda Fanta please," placing an order to the barman.

Dad does not want to drink and drive. While the barman was handing out the drinks.

"It's Always best to keep a clear head" dad explained. Service with a smile."

The barman wiped the bar with a white cloth. Then flicked a white T-towel over his arm and carried on serving the drinks in a flamboyant manner. Oh, these drinks were so refreshing it did not take long for us to drink all of them. Including this Dad politely mentioned cum on children if, we are going to make it's on time to the next hotel we must leave now. We all turned around and started to walk out the door down the corridor into a large hall where the floors were all marble and highly polished. Everywhere where you've looked was perfection.

We walked past the doors of the lifts, just as they were opening a very classy lady and a small puppy that she was carrying in her arms walking out of the lift. Oh, so cute Denise said.

The woman looked down at Denise and smiled but did not stop walking click, click click; click the heels went as she strolled unwaveringly across the marble into the foyer. The sun was beaming through the glass doors as we approached them and steadily walked out down the steps back to the car. Quickly children let's go everybody hopped into the car a little bit of an argument broke out between us Denise and I., which I wanted to sit in the front seat, but as you well inquire Amanda wins again.

The engine burst into life. Those few moments while we were in the hotel the Car must have reached the temperatures in excess of 90° inside the vehicle. As we instantly perspire and struggling to wind down the windows as dad was pulling away. To the junction, looking left and right. Plus steadily dropping onto the main road. We were all amazed at the fascinating views of the main streets that we could see. The architecture was very Georgian looking.

It seemed to be a very nice looking town. But it only took a few minutes, furthermore before we knew it; we have driven through the town we were soon back out into the bush on the main road. Father have driven us straight through the Small town in minutes. Dad seriously wanted to put some distance between the police car accident and his precious children. As any good parent would.

Leading up to 80 miles an hour dad's favourite cruising speed. The conversation in the car at that time was solemn. Like in the back of our minds, there was a madman loose and quite possibly heading towards their town. So we thought about it.

But. Denise did not take long thinking up this idea having a great idea to start a song. About,

three little angels.

Denise came up with his excellent idea to start jamming a new song, and we all joined in to develop this little melody.

"of which one is now sharing with you,"©

"three Little Angels all dressed in white,"♫♫♪♩b♯

♫♫ "this is how it goes learn this and impress your friends."♪♩
♯♪♩♫Three little angels,
All dressed in white,

Trying to get to heaven
On the end of a kite.
but the kite string was broken,
down they all fail.♫♭

♪♪they couldn't get to heaven
so They all went to…♫♫

♫♫Two little angels,
All dressed in Green,
Trying to get to heaven
On the end of a Bean.
but the Beanstalk was broken,
down they all fell.♫♪

♫♪they couldn't get to heaven
so They all went to…♭♫

♪♪One little angel,
he was dressed in white,
Trying to get to heaven
On the end of a bed.
but the bed knob was broken,
down he fell.
he couldn't get to heaven
so They all went to…♫♭

♫Three little devils,
All dressed in red,
Trying to get to heaven
On the end of a thread.
but thread was broken
down they all fell.
Instead of going to heaven
They all went to...♫

♪Two little devils,
All dressed in red,
Trying to get to heaven
On the end of a rocket.
the rocket went bang
down they all fell.
they couldn't get to heaven
so They all went to...♫

♫One little devil,
she was dressed in red,
Trying to get to heaven
On the end of a bed.
but the bed knob was broken,
down she fell.
she couldn't get to heaven
so They all went to..♩.
don't be mistaken don't be misled
they can get to heaven so they

♪ all went to bed!♫#©

"So the song goes on. To turn into a fabulous little song with Devils Angels who are all travelling in different vehicles And different uniforms and circumstances with imagination to get to heaven. Make all the characters up from members of your family you want. But make this song catchy."

This song has managed to travel to the schools as a hit with young children.

I give my sister the credit in starting this song "well-done sister."

''You can imagine how wonderfully exciting the song is when you have to remember what Angel was where and how the angels fell."

a pleasant, happy distraction from Denise

Well, this song has always lifted our spirits.

Bringing smiles to the family plus cheering us all up as we sang it. It's just perfect for us so nicely while we are all singing at the top of our voices. Raising our spirits, You can see that we are all triumphal singing. Happy families again.

('taking our mind off the killer at large')

Rainbow Lodge Hotel

Carefree and worry free at the moment and then suddenly we approach the hotel turning. The car slowed down considerably. Turning off the smooth tarmac road, onto a bumpy dirt track. We all thought this was not going to be as grand as the last hotel that was in the town over 80 miles ago. As this hotel was in the bush. As we approach in the car on a red dirt road, the singing stopped.

Dad pointed towards the brightly colored painted rainbow sign on the edge of the road from the hotel ("100 Meters to Rainbow Lodge Hotel") as dad was reading this out loud. As we drove through the gates, There was just one white public shelter type building surrounded by lots of little thatched huts. They are circular with thatched roofs.

Denise said, "loved them they seem so cute."

The doors of the huts were made out of thin wooden planks with black metal hinges.

"Those huts are stood Just made out of the mud and straw," and thin would Nicely done I must say but not very secure was the thought on my mind. These huts were surrounded by primates, and there is a lovely little kitten cat that greets us.

As we parked the car while walking Across the car park to the main building. The little cat. "oh so cute" the girls made plenty of fuss with this little cat.

His markings were quite unusual As he was smoky grey and black; we could see he had the shape of a diamond on his back a Black Diamond on a pale background.

A very friendly fellow, such distinguishing markings. We all must say; you can see this cat had a very honest personality he was approximately one-year-old so you could say in a loose manner of speaking that he was still a kitten. So cute this little fluffy fellow and so friendly Amanda and Denise made friends with a little kitten almost straight away the little fellow with a diamond on his back made friends with all the children instantly.

The personality and smiles and good feelings that he gave to the family was a welcoming, homely atmosphere of magical hospitality from this little fellow's personality. We could see the Beautiful sunset through the windows behind the counter. As it was about 6 P.m.

dad asked the hotelier. "Confirmation of the Two rooms booked From Mitchell Cotts."

The hotelier said politely "Yes, sir. (ja meneer (in Afrikaans).

And handed dad two keys out with a friendly smile.

Then glancing over to a small cat walking up and down the counter while being fostered by the two girls little cat Was purring it resembled like he had a smile on his furry face. Certainly the two girls did.

This little fellow was a pleasant distraction Rainbow Lodge was the name of the hotel. There was a small carving of a rainbow on each key ring.

We all thought furthermore mention that this is a lovely name for this hotel. The African hotelier said while pointing down the road. You are in the rainbow woods area. Then the hotelier said out the door to the left. Towards the huts. Also said, "Ek kan sien jou baie vriendelik en ons kat se naam is Little Diamond se. Sal jy kyk na hom vanaand as jy bly in sy hut." (translated ("I can see your very friendly and our cat's name is Little Diamond's. Will you look after him tonight as you are staying in his hut.")

While he was looking at the children. All the children came to life with a happy thought on their minds. As we ran to our hotel hut's to explore.

Dad was walking slowly not even attempting to run. I heard him mention about "Bates's Motel" (from a well-known television horror movie) (without prejudice) as I passed father was focusing on my objective on the small thatched dwellings.

Dad muttered to himself. He was walking steadily; his body language was saying everything (not happy). Looking at the state this hotel.

Father said, "It was quaint" Thinking of yourself just keeping the children happy. While approaching the shantytown huts Now let me have a look at these places as we approached the small mud hut and opened the doors with a creek.

Dad said, "A fragile door made out of wooden planks not very safe. Plus that, this door is unlocked already. Right children we will all have to sleep together in this hut."

The girls spoke out, "Oh, know dad, please, please. Let us sleep in our rooms."

Farther back down and said, "Okay, Let us explore our rooms."

"Tom your Sharing father's cabin." There were two single beds made out of wooden planks and one wardrobe with a dirty curtain hanging in front of it on a piece of wire. Above the beds, there was a mosquito nett for each bed. Additionally a small bedside table with a candle On each table.

You can say that this hotel cabin is relatively sparsely furnished. There was no paint on the walls it was dull reddish-brown mud walls. You could see the thatched roof from within the mud hut while looking up at the ceiling. But Tom liked it. It was an adventure.

Dad stamped on the wooden plank floor, (bang bang) shocking Tom for a moment as He was not expecting the sudden noise while looking up in the air. While He was taking in the atmosphere looking at the unusual ceiling that Tom had never seen anything like this before. "It was quite exciting" chicken wire and straw together with about four main supporting beams. Then father looked around to see if there are any animals in here. While Tom was still exploring the hut. You could hear the monkeys outside it seemed like they were laughing at us. As I examined the room with my eyes standing still in the center of this sparsely decorated hut within the Rainbow Lodge campus.

Tom had a familiar feeling and did not feel scared at all he felt that homely feeling as if you have been away from his house for a long time. A feeling of familiarity came over Tom. A happy but sad feeling of contentment. Is this the sort of place that Tom used to live in his past life. Here is the sort of feeling that he had. There was unquestionably something magical about this dwelling. That triggered off distant subconscious memories.

Dad muttered to himself "Bates Motel" quietly to himself. While he was distracted looking for unwanted lodgers in the hut. There was a Quiet noise at the door. As the rusty hinges on the door slightly squeaked, and a face of this little grey cat appeared around the door, I mentioned nothing in the hope that the cat would come fully into the room. Of which he did.

Tom felt so pleased that he had chosen this hut. Just as the hotelier said earlier. (Please look after my cat as he sleeps in your hut.) The little cat walked quietly across the room and under Tom's bed and disappeared. You could hear the girls settling in next door as they were talking. And they just seemed so happy.

Tom steadily walked over to his bed and sat down. As his dad was striking a match, we could see a small puff of smoke rise from the crackling match head.

As his Dad decided to light a candle. Fizzing popping and crackling went the wick, the smell of the burning match and paraffin candle started to fill the room. Accompanied by the light as it is growing as the flames took hold of the Candlewick. The room little with the Golden Glow dads shadow grew as the candle flame got brighter.

Dad turned around shaking the match in his hand and placing it in the ashtray that was also on the table side of the bed. Then taking out an individual second match from the matchbox. As he walked over to my bed at the same time striking a 2nd match with only one or 2 strides before he was standing at my bedside table holding the match close to the candle wick. A Moment later the Candlewick fizzed crackled as the flame struggled to stay alight.

Dad caressed the Candlewick with the match to encourage the fire to burn brightly. The fire climbed into the air about an inch Dad held the match away from the burning candle wick. Furthermore, then he stepped forward with a burning match in his hand and said, Son would you like to blow this match out son. (Once again looking directly into my eyes) I acknowledged by taking a deep breath including pursing my lips to give as much power to the wind that I was about to produce. Blowing his fathers match out. First Inhaling through his flared nostrils. Then paused for what seemed adjusting his aim like an a 2nd before Tom exhaled and blew out the match. Father smiled. Then turned around and flipped the match out of his hand. Strode towards the ashtray. That was against the side of his bed. Which spanned through the air across the room? Moreover bounced off the edge of the ashtray clipping a cigarette butt that he had smoked earlier spinning around then landing in the middle of the ashtray.

tom said, "What a shot I said to dad."

Dad turned back looked at me face-to-face smiles and said, "that's how it's done Son" I must say it was a pretty amazing shot, with accuracy and skill.

Dad. He was always impressive with things like that. By this time, both candles continued growing to their full strength with the light filling the room.

The girls called out from next door. "What are your rooms like"? "We will be with you in a moment," said dad. Naturally the girls couldn't wait any longer. Then they came around to visit our room because my father and I were sitting down. On our Beds interrupted what seemed to be an interesting conversation between us you could say it was Father and son bonding. I was enjoying it before I was interrupted by the door opening and the two girls walking in.

Father immediately said, "coming girls." As we prepare for another little family meeting to find out what the evening would entail. As their father was quite tired after a long drive, it was not going to be a late-night as dad mentioned. "We are going out to a bistro to find something tasty to eat.

Are you all interested and hungry" father said. "Yes, we are" all the children mentioned together. Then at that moment a little Head popped out from underneath my bed; Plus Amanda paid attention to this and started stroking the cat. Amanda says "can we have the cat in our hut, please."

"No! The cat is not going to be in anybody's hurt. The Cat is going to be staying outside."

"Yes, but Dad."

"no Amanda the cat stays outside I'm sure he has somewhere to stay."

Naturally Right at the beginning father had misheard that we were surprisingly staying in the Cat's home. The two children look to us thinking there must be a way of smuggling the cat into my hut. Amanda imagined this Tom felt this and also Denise thought this too. The father was adamant that this cat Was not stopping in this hut or the girls stab at. Wright children let's get going. So Father he said. Standing to walking across the room. Furthermore picking up the little cat placing him out of the door followed by three children and my father as he locked the door behind us. All 4 of us jump into the car. after further knocked the girl door also Denise knowing full well that her plan was foiled. In getting the little diamond cat back into her room.

Who was to know what was going to unfold later on from our actions.

A full-service restaurant and Bistro?

Driving down a dirt road to the bistro restaurant, it was very dark riding through the bush. Then suddenly all of us could see lights through the trees.

"Hopefully, not too long from now."

Father said so. Then suddenly a black shadow ran across the front of the car, it was not small it was About the size of a dear.

Dad slammed on the anchors breaking as suddenly as possible; the car skidded a little bit. Then the animal, but it has already disappeared into the bush as if by magic it was their one 2nd and gone the next

Dad corrected the car as quickly as possible and carried on driving. That was a close shave. He said is everyone all right. "Wow, what was that."

Amanda shouted hysterically.

We still don't know what happened. To this day. What was it? However, it was clearly very fast. One more corner on the dirt road. We arrived at the bistro restaurant.

Now this was a gorgeous place nestled in the Bush dad said.

There were tables outside underneath the shelter of the thatched porch roof and people already sitting down it seemed to be quite a rustic divine place providing a gathering of like-minded, friendly people. Also, we were surrounded by, guards there. Looking after the security of the guests dining in the Lodge restaurant. All of us walked together along the full wooden plank decking. The family and I were aware of a romantic table setting. Outside under the thatched porch roof under the stars.

Ours, The waiter, lit the candle for us. Giving the table a warming Golden Glow the Waiter was showing us professional hospitality.

Asking Father "from which menu he would like to order from Sir."

After helping us all to our seats.

The large porch area comprised sheltered with a large straw thatched roof.

"Drinks first."

Dad orders his drink and then orders the children's usual "Coca-Cola and two fanter's, please." That gave us freedom to look over the menu.

Dad wanted something quick because he was hungry so went for a special on the menu. "Crocodile steaks," he mentioned. Now you do not see this on the card very often, so we all tried it. Well, what can I say What a fabulous treat of crocodile steaks?

The Waiter said that all crocodile meat is positively bred free range within 5 km of the restaurant healthily. The stakes did not take too long as we were talking among ourselves about the experience's so far of our journey.

Dad was worried about the Rainbow Lodge hotel. As the building was not very secure, and the worry of this escaped convict armed and dangerous at large.

Plus the attention of this wild animal that jumped in front of them moving car just moments before. Less than 5 km away from the Rainbow Lodge but large enough as the animal was heading in a different direction from our minimalistic sparse hotel accommodation.

You can tell that we were in the bush because the music from the crickets were very loud.

the atmosphere was very genteel.

Soon The waiter turned up with full plates balancing on his arms. Soon followed by another Waiter, who came out with knives and forks. The stakes looked delicious and enormous on the plate. We all ate a bit it tasted like fish and the texture of chicken. However, it was delicious oh so pleasant and warmed our spirits. As we had a very nice conversation over our evening meal about the journey of our holiday.

The excitement of this holiday is unfolding day by day.

Then suddenly without any warning we heard a

loud roar it seems quite close to the restaurant.

The people on the Table mentioned that there was a pride of lions in the area.

As we are not far from a local drinking waterhole where the animals all congregate for their water.

Don't worry The man said. The guards around the bistro restaurant are armed, and their Training will keep us all safe as they do their job well. Also, the lights insistence keep the large cats away. (muttered under his breath as long as the generator does not stop)

We automatically thought that the animal ran out in front of us was probably trying to escape from the Lions. We all found this rather amusing as we are enjoying our crocodile steaks. Feeling reasonably safe with all the security around us. It remained a beautiful clear night we could see every star in the sky.

That was just such a fabulous place to be the people were so friendly, and the service was excellent, so we stayed here for some time before heading back to the Rainbow Lodge hotel. Scary hotel. Bates's Rainbow Lodge dad says.

We are all thinking now about these lines bursting into the Hut through the flimsy wooden doors.

Dad says, "Tom stop talking about that you will scare the girls." Amanda stares at me as she usually does.

So squinting her eyes slightly just to intimidate me. However, this moment in time I ignored her as I usually do. (Sibling rivalry.)

Denise was poking around the crocodile steak. I do not suppose she enjoyed it so much as we all did.

Denise left the last chunk of crocodile steaks on her plate when everybody else has finished. dessert.

Dad says. "Fantastic. Coconut ice cream in the jungle Looks at exactly what it says on the menu. So sweet and tasty. Oh! Yes, we will all have one of them each."

Here is the article as it appeared in the bowl before me. It had a hot coating of dark chocolate drizzled over the top that the ice cream have frozen the chocolate slightly. It just made such a lovely cracking noise as you push your fork and spoon into the ice cream. Yummy. Oh, so delicious

Tom speaks: I suppose I will never eat ice cream like that again. Another round of drinks just finished the meal off nicely. Also, the sound of the crickets still playing their song you can say it would be a romantic atmosphere and a place that I would love to visit one day soon again.

Father had managed to strike up a conversation with the next table as they were interested in us.

"Where are all of you from?" Maintained to be one of the questions?

Dad explained "his children have just come over from the UK, and we are on a holiday expedition."

"Are you going to be visiting the Safari Park?"

Dad "No, this is not feasible for the family at the moment."

The man laughed and said "you are in the Safari Park at the moment. It is just about half a kilometre down this road to into the main entrance of the Safari this is where you begin. We all work and live there. Hereabouts is our local hangout restaurant bar."

Tom asked, "how long have you worked and lived out in the safari park and Bush."

A Man said. "I am on my 5th year I'm the One how looks after most of the game on the reserve. All the game hunting and seasonal culling, etc."

Amanda was just finishing off the last spoonful of ice cream when she heard the words from the man as he said culling. You could see that she was shocked at the expression on her face as then she dropped the dessert spoon back in the bowl without finishing off that last mouthful of coconut ice cream.

Tom: could understand that she is a little bit upset about the animals being killed.

Even though Denise just munched hear way through an 18 ounce crocodile steak, just mouthfuls left to say too much.

However, he said "yes!"

Oh then suddenly everybody looks up to take notice. Looking at a Man wearing khaki green clothes his shorts with ankle high walking boots on.

Moments before the commencement of an incredible story.

Dad mentioned, "have you had any close shaves with wild animals?"

Not expecting much of the narration from the man.

The hunter-man spoke out exactly this story What just happened?

Said the hunter. "He was down by the water hole where there was a local tribe washing their clothes. There was a The Young girl on the bank just collecting water to sprinkle on her clothes while washing them On the rocks. Suddenly there was a surge in the water. Amazingly a part of a split-second later, I saw the pearly white teeth. also the jaws of a crocodile lunging powerfully out of the still water. A water wave towards the young girl, immediately the water splash violently, as the crocodile battled to take the child into the water. Know Time to think just act, instantly while the beast crocodile. Is acutely Grabbing the young girl by her left leg Instantly sweeping her off her feet. She landed hard on the sloping slippy muddy bank. While trying to pull kicking and screaming terrified young girl into the water. The girl She immediately screamed at the top of her lungs. Foreseeing this incident I was close enough to jump from the bank on top of the crocodile's body. Surprisingly, the crocodile opened his mouth to go for a 2nd bite of a young child so violent that was. I managed to pull the girl's leg free, from the jaws of this deadly monster. Although I was, still on top. Of the bull crocodile holding the jaws of this huge crocodile shot with both hands, I was lying on top of his body at that time. Trying to cover his eyes. Then the crocodile flipped over using his powerful tale. I just lost my grip at that moment as the crocodile shook his head left and right and then spun me around effortlessly into mid air. Landing back into the water, I could not have held onto him any longer. As he was so powerful, he got the better of me that fast evil crocodile. Also, at the same time in midair he bit deep and hard into my right leg, the crocodile began to spin in the water. I went under holding my breath frantically grabbing for anything that I could get my hands-on. Just managing to grab my knife while I was still spinning under in and out of the water catching a desperate breath whenever I can. Including pushing and stabbing the knife into the crocodile. Anything that I could stab-at. The water at this time was red with my blood, and the crocodiles power made me feel like a rag doll. The locals because they were nearby managed to grab my arms plus hold on tight them Pulling me into the bank. An amazing old lady started bashing the crocodile over the head with a Cast-iron frying pan aggressively. Thankfully the crocodiles ceased its death roll. Also, ripped off some bits from my leg. As the locals pulled me to safety on the bank After a human chain tug-of-war With life and death gamble with one man eating bull crocodile in the waterhole."

Denise said, "Oh my you are so lucky to be alive!"

Three children with my father were sitting there with their mouths wide open after listening to such a close shave, of clear and present death. Of a heroic man who saved the life of a young girl that day.

This man showed us the scars on his right leg. They were large bite marks and chunks of flesh ripped out of both legs. You could see how deep the wounds were. As the skin just covered the bone. "It took me three years to recover. From that," the man said. "However, I feel fully fit now. I always carry a gun with me, when I go near the water. The crocodile was hunted down afterwards as it was, well known that this crocodile was over 28 feet in length and usually when they grow to such a size they are class as a man-eater. So when they get about 20 feet long at the farm, they are often slaughtered, and the meat is sold off. To help support, the welfare of the game reserve." "That is so interesting," Tom said.

You truly are a hero. He said loudly and clearly. The man smiled and gave Tom a wink.

Everybody around the tables had been listening to everything that has occurred. The man mentioned his name, and to this day I cannot remember what his name was. However, the other man that he was sitting with him his named Bob Irwin but to this day I still think that he is a very brave man from saving that young girls life. With no thought to it. Of the consequences to his own-life-and-well-being. In my eyes, in my book. That is a superhero story. My father bought the man a bottle of beer he replied "I do not usually drink on this occasion, I will Cheers and thank very much." Additionally father said, "you deserve that for sharing the experiences and entertaining us of your near death encounter."

"The gentleman said thanked you very much you are welcome." Then Dad said, "children it is time for us to leave as we need to get back to the Rainbow Lodge." The man said, "Rainbow Lodge?"

dad said. "yes."

"Do you know anything about this Rainbow Lodge?" The man looked at the children individually and said., "yes I do. Oh dear, a thought came to our minds. Thinking that there is going to be another horror story unfolding at any moment. The man said it was a gorgeous place in the morning. However, the primates are a bit aggressive. Make sure everything stays secured away, and you would always firmly closed the door. Alternatively, else the monkeys will be in your room."

"Oh, okay" father said, "Thank you for your helpful advice. We will get on, and maybe we will see you in the future. Take care of yourselves. Also, good night."

As we all left the table, we said to everybody "good night."

I remember that evening went so well we could have remained there for another couple of hours and watch the sunrise.

However, dad was an adamant that he needed some rest. So this implied time for us to leave.

Dad paid the waiter giving him a handsome tip.

We piled in the car off we went. Driving the 5 km back to the Rainbow Lodge hotel. Within moments, we could see the rainbow Lodge appearing in the darkness as we pulled up and floodlit the area with the car headlamps. Those solitude huts did not appear very appealing in the pitch black night. Also, it seemed quite scary. However, dad parked the car very close to the huts.

Dad said to us "if anything goes wrong makes sure that you get in the car do not run off into the bush." Okay, dad said this with a smile on everyone's faces thinking that he was joking.

However, knowing it was enough serious. Well, after getting out of the car also making our way into our little huts. We visited each other's huts.

Father lit the candles in the girl's hut, and then we all said good night. Then my father and I went off to our hut.

Both huts were pretty much identically laid out and sparsely decorated.

Tom lay down on one's bed pulling his mosquito netting around his bed and looking up into the mosquito netting it seemed so relaxing. Also, soon he felt the weight of his body sinking into the mattress with comfort and relaxing feelings. Along with a happy feeling over him. I am tired and ready to go to sleep.

Dad said, "good night." Tom.

Tom said, "good night father sweet dreams see you in the morning. Good night everybody!"

The girls called out from next-door "good night dad good night Tom." Dad and Tom replied.

"Goodnight"

Amanda "good night."

Denise and everybody shouted out together "good night."

Dad leaned outside these mosquito net And snubbed the candle out with his thumb and forefinger.

Instantly darkness prevailed within the hut; the silence came with it. All that we could here be the crickets. Just for a short time. Occasionally y'all could hear the animals outside.

However, then suddenly the against a stark reminder that we are in the wilds on the edge of the jungle or thou would say the Bush. Surrounded by wild animals as there was a piercing squeal. Moreover, y' all could hear monkeys were fighting each other there was a significant fight going on outside the doors.

Dad called out to the girls; "Are yourself okay is everything all right."

The girls squealed out; and said "this is happening on our doorstep we think the cat is fighting with the monkeys." "Is your door closed nice and safe."

Father call out?

"Oh yes, dad it is safely locked. We also have the cupboards up against the door."

"Good girls stay there, and you will be safe."

Also, as quick as it started the noise dissipated of the struggling animals outside the girl's door.

Before knowing it with this deadly quiet. Then suddenly a ball of light came through the wall and shot straight up and through the ceiling of the hut. Dad says "put that torch light out son," Tom said nothing. As the light disappeared. Lay silently In bed looking up into the mosquito net eyes fixed in the position of the point where the unusual spiritual light went into the pitch black ceiling fixed eyes fixed on this point. A tranquil feeling came over oneself for one had seen this effect before. Giving a little prayer to help the traumatic unfortunate passing of this departing animal spirit. Still not knowing what creature for an animal has passed at this moment. He was putting 2 and two together from the noise and conflict that was outside the hut's, relaxed atmosphere followed and piece, Tom fell asleep. Waking up in the morning with the sunshine beaming through the cracks in the wooden door panels. It felt so comfortable sleep in this bed looking through the mosquito netting was dominating the bed furthermore looking and seeing one's father lying on his bed surrounded by the sunlight and mosquito netting as well.

Gave to oneself a warm and fuzzy spiritual feeling. We know that these huts were rough. But it was an experience worth indulging in as it gave Tom; the sensation of going back to his happy roots and back in time. The experience of life that evening. Also, this morning he went through many feelings to learn for the future and his faith. Dad jumped out of bed to answer. Speaking Cheerfully out; "good morning Tom. Are you awake?"

Tom, "oh yes that I am Dad. Good morning father" "good morning. Did you sleep well."

Did Tom say? "No, Tom. However, I am sure I got my quotes worth."

"I know how you feel."

Tom said. "I am sure everything will be going fine today."

"Do you really think, so?"

Did Dad say? "Yes, I am enjoying this time with you very much."

The conversation ticked along nicely this morning we both paid thanks to each of us for a holiday experience.

Dad placed his feet on the floor wiggling his toes while he was sitting on the edge of the bed, then dad asked the question, "Tom I didn't know you had a torch light."

tom, "No, I don't have one."

Tom said. "Something came into the room last night You must have seen it because it let the room up."

Silence came over the room while dad looks down just preparing to get up. Pulling out the socks from within his shoes and Checking his footwear by giving them a bang on the side of the bed. Dad said "it's just one of them unexplained phenomena on"

Tom: That becomes when he thought to personally to oneself. If he had done that. He would not have murdered that Innocent cockroach in his boot. The morning after us had landed that only happened a few nights ago.

However, thankfully the evening before I had copied my dad with the socks in the shoes.

Dad stood up out of bed walked slowly to the door only a few strides as the hut was so small. To the door giving his self the early morning stretch.

Dad lit up a Rothmans Royals cigarette, with his stainless steel Ronson-via flame lighter. Of which he got for his 21st birthday present from my grandma and grandpa.

Dad took a large draw off the cigarette and blew a large smoke ring across the room. It floated through the air with no effort a tall towards Tom's bed of which father hit his target accurately on target he purposely crashed the smoke ring into Tom's mosquito net. The smoke rolled down the outside of the net resembling a small smoky waterfall.

It looked interestingly beautiful Tom stared at the cascade of smoke, rolling down the mosquito net. Unusually, Tom realises that the smoke was not penetrating through the mosquito net. What could have caused this he thought this to oneself.

Also, then asked the question dad, "why does the smoke not penetrate through the net."

Father answered "very interesting point you had their son. As this is to do with air pressure and the size of the modules in the smoke. This method has been used in the coal mines believe it or not son."

Tom said. "Oh yes I believe it Dad,"

"son it is called the Davy lamp method we have this little conversation while Tom was getting dressed.

Dad explained about The Davy lamp is a protection light for control in combustible atmospheres, consisting of a candlewick lamp with the flame contained within a thin mesh screen. It transpired designed in 1815 by Sir Humphry Davy. Initially burned vegetable oil. It was constructed for use in coal mines or, newly named the pits to reducing the danger of explosions. Due to the presence of methane plus other flammable gases, called firedamp or mine damp.

Sir Humphry Davy had discovered that a fire contained within a mesh of a specified fineness cannot ignite firedamp. This shield acts as a fire arrestor; air (& any firedamp present) can pass through the mesh quickly complete to support flaming. Simply the narrow holes are too little to allow the flame to diffuse through them also ignite any firedamp outside the mesh. Thus enabling the light showing through the mesh giving the coal miners light in their darkest needs in the pitch black of the coal mines in the 18th century.

Tom, one you are a smart young man" (father said) "to notice something like that. One's mind works in an extraordinary way." Tom sat on his bed listening to every word his father said.

Right there, Dad told him that he is going out to see the girls are okay. "Coming back soon?" Father mentioned.

"Oh yes," Tom said. Within moments, Tom jumped up out of bed copying the same ritual as his father except for the smoking.

Dad said this. "are you joining come along with us son.

We stepped out of the small door one at a time and down the steps. Out of the hut, greeted by the early morning sunrise. Casting long shadows on the ground through the trees. Fresh, crisp air was the so welcoming Magic hour, (if you happened to be a photographer you would understand it) as the early morning sun blazed a trail for the adventurous new day. It did not take long for the adventure to start.

Tom noticed or so he thought.

Since the cat left two little presents on the doorstep of his sisters. Traditional mud hut. (You know that the presence

that your pet Leaves you after a long evening of hunting)
Well, on the step there are two fluffy little packages. So not
taking too much notice at this point until, father and Tom
stepped closer to the mud hut together. As Daddy knocked
the door and said hello girls, are you already.

The Girls replied nearly father just coming out. We could
hear the bedside tables being pushed away from the opposite
side of this door the girls small barricade is being dismantled.
Then moments later the door opened

Denise was the first person out of two sisters to come to
the door. (I so wish it had not been Denise. To see this)
However, as Denise smiled spoke good morning Tom.

Tom looked down realising the horror and sorrow on the
doorstep where she stood.

Denise followed Tom's eyes. Both were realising together
that these little fluffy parcels were not a mouse gift from
the cat. However, they were a gift from the carnivorous
monkeys. Also, each and every think of the cat. Except for
his to back, paws had been surgically severed on the joints by
the horrible predatory animals and also nothing remaining
of the cat's carcass just leaving too soft little paws on the
doorstep. With not leaving any other remaining evidence
of the unfortunate dismembered pussycat

Oh, the horror of this was so unbearable for Denise.

Denise: speaking and crying at the same time just saying. "The poor cat had lost his life on the doorstep Weeping, and all of us have heard his demise Under 8 hours ago. None of us totally realised at the time when this little cat was struggling for its life was being attacked and ripped to pieces by a mob of carnivorous monkeys!" The latest few moments of the life of this cat WAS listen to like a fight for life and death. Including then in this suffering cats moment by the family the struggle we will never forget. Of which one of his last nine lives continue immortalised in the memories of the people who read this book.

If yourself sense, something rubbing up against your leg while you are reading this passage do not despair, it is just a little Neil Diamond without prejudice just saying hello to you. That is Neil Diamond saying hello as this is his name.

tribute to Neil Diamond and the memories of his wonderful loving personality.

The Cat that have been eaten by the monkeys in the early hours of this morning. What remained of this little fluffy cat was his two back paws. Well, one thought personally Oh my!. That is just so terrible. Just before we managed to move these two pause. From that little fluffy, friendly cat, Denise opened the door and looked, about to step outside. Dad said stop. As Denise looked down and seen the cat two back paws lying there amputated from the body of that lovely cat that we have seen the night before its death.

Denise just inhaled and then stood there screaming out within a blind panic, she was that loud. People appeared out of the hut to see what was going on.

Denise is still hysterically screaming. So rightly so.

Tom ran over to the doorstep and grabbed hold of the cat's pores to protect his sister's feelings. So he immediately threw them away outside away from the hut. They felt so soft fluffy and light in Tom's hands as the through them away from his sister and out of sight.

Dad immediately caught hold of Tom. So said, do not put your hands Near your face as you need to go and wash them straight away.

Tom did specifically what his father said to him. Immediately went away to wash his hands.

Dad walked up the steps to Denise and gave her a big hug consoling her instantly. Amanda? What has happened so far?

Denise began to tell her but then started to burst into tears again the tears were relentless as she balled her eyes out.

As Tom came back from the toilets after washing his hands, everybody was sitting in the car waiting to go.

Tom said, "Take us away from this horrible place! Please!" after jumping Into the back seat, started sliding his self forward; holding onto the front seat looking over the shoulders of the driver; passenger. We are all Listening to a song on dad's tape recorder. Without prejudice. Hello, my friend hello was the song. From Neil Diamond.

THEIR father did not spare any time accelerating away as this incident of the monkeys hurt the family and his daughters. You could tell dad was not happy at all. So still in a terrible state of shock the whole family. Drove carefully out of the car park as the gates were relatively narrow.

That just added such another painful blow to the family in the car, when we seen one of the very vicious monkeys sitting on the gatepost. Giving us plainly such an evil grin as if this monkey Happened to have an evil intelligence. When we got alongside the gatepost, the primate punched the car window. While Holding the severed's tale of a cat in the primates hand at the same time also screeched a piercing cry as loud as he could. This piercing shriek of evilness echoed through the car and our memories of the night to this day.

Dad Raged up and said with a growl in his voice. "If one had one's gun to hand, one would have turned down the window and shot that evil possessed monkey in the head."

Dad looked carefully down the road preparing for an accelerated getaway moreover was pulling away out of the Rainbow Lodge car park at that time Denise and Amanda just realised what the monkey had in his hand. As the dirty, bloodstained Mark on the window from where the monkey had just punched, it was still there. Again they screened and burst into tears.

Tom was also very upset with this incident.

Tom said Diamond is in heaven now. Trying to constrain his sister

Dad spoke out don't worry children I promise you; we will never go to a place like that again. We are all very assured of this if we had Of stopped there for another night something serious would have happened to one of us or if not all of us. In that terrible place. Rainbow Lodge, where that little diamond cat had Lost his life. So shameful of the night before. Us a little bit more thought on our behalf we could have saved little cat Neil Diamonds life.

But instead now we are sitting in silence listening to music on the stereo of Neil Diamond the singer singing.

As the family are breaking loose! While Attempting to cope with their thoughts. Reminiscences of seeing hearing An act of atrocious cruelty of the cat tiny Neil Diamond, the girls, was crying, and the men were straining to hold back their tears. Quietly listening To dads favourite music on the road.

99 miles from Victoria Falls

We have been driving for a while Father looks down and asks Denise for the map; Denise handed over to Amanda. Father asks for the nearest town. Okay, father. Amanda said.

It's not far it's only an inch Amanda says. One inch dad says. Oh, dear dimensions. And the expression on his face looks a bit worried. Amanda says what's wrong dad.

Dad says don't worry we are looking for a petrol station. I'm not quite on a red yet, but it won't be long at this speed. Amanda worked it out the next town is 20 miles away. I'm sure we don't imagine that says.

Father pulls out his flask from down this side of the car seat. And hands it over to Amanda. Amanda unscrews one cup from the top of the container. Also begins to pour careful dad a small cup of coffee. The steam floated out of the flask we can all smell the fresh coffee.

Amanda handed the coffee over to her father. Father took an extended sipped the hot refreshing coffee. Furthermore handed it back to Amanda. Amanda also takes a sip. Then Amanda handed the piping hot coffee over to the backseat where Tom was impatiently waiting for a nice long tasty drink of the hot fresh coffee. Tom turns around to Denise. Who is asleep with boredom and impression of the monkey that killed little diamond, Tom gives Denise a tiny bit of thoughtful encouragement to wake his sister up.

Denise opened one eye, upon immediately noticing the cup of hot coffee opens both eyes and smiled refreshingly. To Tom.

Denise gently takes the coffee cup out of Tom's hand; she took a long sip of the fresh coffee and handed back to Tom. Tom gave up the cup to his dad, and his dad took another sip and placed the coffee cup back on the center console near the handbrake.

The memories of the evening before was still on the family's mind but not dwelling on the past too much.

quietly thinking to themselves about sorrow while They are all Looking at the view down the long hill through the hot tropical heat-hays that seemed to stretch for miles down the road.

The heat was Making a silver mirage that only looked like a lake; it was truly amazing because this is the biggest illusion that the whole family had ever seen Just over those hills is our next town. And where we need to fill up with petrol. These 20 mints passed very rapidly as before we know it, we were pulling onto a petrol station forecourt. As we stopped, and African gentleman appeared and asked the father if he had been travelling long. The father said yes, we had.

The gentleman manservant "where are you off to" Dad said we just need some petrol please as we are going to Victoria Falls.

The African gentleman said, "can you pull forward to this petrol pump."

Whatever unusual manner, since we happened to be lined up at the petrol pump already as father wanted four-star petrol for the car

The African gentleman waved us forward to the next pump and started to fill the car.

He asked how "much fuel would you like Sir."

Father said, "Fill her up, please!"

The African gentleman filled the car with petrol and cleaned the windscreen.

So father gave him a tip.

Then we drove off to the final leg of the journey. Dad Announced about the interesting historical place was going to visit.

as we only have an hour's drive left before we reach Victoria Falls our shortstop destination before the family goes over the border to Rhodesia

We are all quite excited because this is a traditional African hotel resort. Tom you will like this because they have weaver birds here.

Tom was getting quite excited about thoughts of seeing the weaver birds. As he was very interested in ornithology, (the study of birds) not long now the hotel was in sight. It's a lovely white single level building with large arches. Dad was just manoeuvring the car, and suddenly the car started to sputter and backfire.

Dad said I can't believe this it is just like we are running out of petrol, but this is impossible surely. Sure enough, before we managed to get to the hotel the car park engine entirely stopped. We had broken down. Nevertheless dad put the clutch in and we were rolling luckily enough it was downhill to the car park. Skilfully father turned the car into the car park and stopped the car. He told us all to wait in the car while he checked the engine. Dad popped the bonnet of the car. Opening the car door and stepping out. While he was walking to the front of the car, he was looking quite worried at this time and looking under the bonnet we could see through the crack underneath the bonnet from inside the car. Dad was shaking his head and checking the HT leads. Then he sat back into the car and tried to start the car again, nothing was happening besides the engine just turning over. (Engine ignition sound of the engine turning over)

Dad said, "thank you this problem is going to need a little bit longer than expected children. So You can all get out of her car and stretch your legs after this long journey now children. But don't go far stay close to the car. It's safe here as we are all in the car park."

Denise and Amanda jumped out of the car and also Tom.

Tom strolled around to the front of the car and started talking to his father questioned him with what is wrong. His father told Tom "I'm not sure what is wrong." (father had a serious look on his face.)

"It appears like there is fuel in the fuel line. Go around and have a look at the exhaust, tell me what you can see Tom,"

"okay dad," Tom said.

After walking around the back of the car, Tom noticed that there was a puddle of dirty black water underneath the exhaust pipe. Tom called out to his father the problem that Tom had seen.

Dad looked at this. Tom said," look what I have found Dad." Toms Father walked around to the back of the car. Tom then pointed out a patch of water under the exhaust pipe as it was also still dripping. "Oh dear well that doesn't look right does it son.

There just appears to be a lot of condensation coming from the exhaust pipe" Tom's father said to him, but to be safe let's investigate.

It was a bright sunny day; furthermore there was no site of any rain or had been that week.'

Tom's father pulled out and crisp white folded handkerchief, out of this top pocket. Embroidered neatly with his father's initials. Then Tom's father wrapped his finger inside his handkerchief. He proceeded to take a Tiny sample of the puddle that had settled underneath the exhaust pipe. On his crisp white handkerchief. Brought this extremely close to his nose to smell the sample. Dad Said, "This does not feel or smell quite right. Tom this doesn't smell like petrol for some reason it doesn't look quite right either. But it has positively come from the exhaust pipe. Come on Tom let's go and investigate the engine." father and son walked round to the front of the car.

Tom's dad asks, "Do you know what this is?" Tom's father stands there pointing under the bonnet Pointing to a piece of clear circular plastic in line with two black pipes? "No? I don't say Tom. Tom returns the question asks "What is it dad it is the fuel filter son," Tom smiled and nodded.

"Can you see the inside of it." Tom climbed onto the bumper with both feet firmly placed on the bumper and leant in towards the engine to get a closer look.

"Oh yes, he said. I Can you see that it looks like there are two different types of liquids in a clear plastic tube."

Tom in a Eureka moment said "yes, of course, is that water?" he said.'s

Dad said, "Do you know what liquid should just be in this?"

Tom said, "Petrol!" "yes," his father said that's what it should be. But it is not is it.

Tom said, "Own Dear." His father said I cannot believe that they have done this."

"What have they done dad Tom? My petrol tank has transpired to occur contaminated with water. So when we filled up with petrol they mixed water in it" innocently Tom said. "Yes!"

"That's right," his father said. "We have been conned!!!! I hope that we have enough petrol in the tank at least to get us all to the next petrol station."

Meanwhile, I'm going to let this settle in the fuel tank as the petrol will float to the surface, and the water will sink. So we can drain off the water from the bottom of the tank and save the petrol. So the longer we leave it more petrol we will collect."

Dad said, "So let's get booked into a hotel as we don't understand how long we are going to be here. And I will get some tools and sort this problem out."

So father locked up the car. Took us to the hotel. Here stood a beautiful hotel, and there was a large complex connected to it. Swimming pools picnic areas and traditional African village with one real African chief that everybody seems to enjoy very much. You can see how the African villagers traditionally prepared and ground the maze up as their staple diet. They were living in the same sort of a mud hut as we stopped at the Rainbow Lodge hotel. Except for the chief and the witch doctor lived in the square hut.

The witchdoctor seems very entertaining, as he was wearing unusual feathers and bones. The witchdoctor was chanting over a tin lid and throwing bones onto it. Father, let us look at the compound. And left somebody with us to look after His children while father fixes the car.

The woman of the hotel. While the father was working on the car. It did not taking too long to get it sorted out he just used a few clear plastic drums to separate the petrol from the water. He told us later on that was very lucky as he had managed to get half a tank of petrol. He said we won't be going backward to that petrol station again. But I'm sure that he made a telephone call back to his company and told the principal director of what happened.

father came back after finishing with the petrol problem with the car and took us round to show us the weaver birds these birds were quite beautiful.

Dad said, "the Weaver birds. Are also known as weaver finches. Getting their name since of their elaborately to woven nests (the most complex of any birds'), though some are well-known for their particular parasitic nesting customs. The nests differ in size, shape, material utilised and construction techniques from species to species. Materials used for building nests include excellent leaf-fibres, hemp, and sprigs. Numerous species weave very fine nests using thin strands of leaf fibre. But some, like the buffalo-weavers, produce massive untidy stick nests in their communities, whichever may have spherical woven nests inside. The weaver bird populations will happen discovered close to water bodies. They sometimes cause crop damage, notably reputed to be the world's most numerous bird."

These nests were amazing as we can get so close and see the skill of these fantastic birds. These birds were so friendly and inquisitive they would hop onto the table where we were sitting. Just stand there looking around the table. Dad rolled up a little piece of tissue paper into a straw shape. And handed out in front of the birds beak the bird flapped his wings and cocked his head over as if he was inspecting the straw that dad had made of his paper napkin. The bird took it in his beak and flew straight up into the air. The weaver bird took flight approximately 10 feet away from the table to a nest that was already in construction. This beautiful bird started to weave in tissue paper straw into the fibres of his own nest. We were all amazed how this bird was acting and how fast it worked with the paper napkin straw. We all love this so much.

So we started to make straws out of paper napkins, and before we know it, the bird came back and took another one, and flew back and forth to his nest. Time and time again he did this as we sat enjoying a meal. You could save his little yellow bird with black markings started to get very friendly with us. And his nest standout from all the other birds nests.

Amanda says, "he would be in trouble if it rains as the paper will go soggy, and his nest will fall to pieces." "Oh! Dear," dad said, "That was a shame. Good thinking, then" said Father. So at that point we will stop making paper straws for the Bird.

This little bird stood on the table for ages flapping his wings waiting for another straw amazingly.

Tom felt quite afraid of these birds because of their tropical markings and there Piercing Red and yellow eyes, Even though, they were very friendly to the family. There was just something there that unsettled Tom with these markings. (making him quite uncomfortable) One suppose his natural instincts were kicking in. From the danger markings on the bird. To scare away natural predators. Therefore, the defence mechanism is that God had given this bird was working. Even though, Tom was not predator to this beautiful bird but Tom was unmistakably in touch with his early warning systems of his spirituality Of his natural gift.

Weaver Birds

Dad says, "three happy children soaking up the sun after eating a fantastic meal with their father in beautiful idyllic settings with friendly tropical birds and very interesting friendly people. It's time to get going". "Shall we have one more last quick look around before we leave?"

"What a lovely idea" agreed the three children.

Tom stood up slowly and asked "dad could leave the table please, just a bathroom break," he says.

father mentioned "secretly."

Truthfully Tom just wanting to remove his self away from the birds. His father lets him walk away up the winding steps to the back of the hotel.

Tom enjoyed this little bit of freedom, as he walked up the steps. He turned round to looked behind him you can see the beautiful setting the downhill this made him feel very tall Tom could see the swimming pools at the bottom of the terraces. With crystal clear water Lots of people enjoying their selves in the sunshine. Especially his sisters Clearly sitting there all together with his father.

Tom turned around and took one step forward not looking where he was going you bumped straight into a young girl about his age.

Tom said, "I'm very sorry." To the young Lady. She says, "that's okay, and it was my fault one was not looking where one was going."

Tom said, "that's my excuse one was not looking either."

The young girl says to Tom. "Isn't this not such a beautiful place." Agreed Tom. "How long are you staying here?" He asked the interesting attractively young girl, "not long" she said with a lovely smile. Looking down at her feet shyly Gently but slowly stroking her ebony colour hair away from her face. As if she was making a picture frame for her beautiful features with her hair.

"We are proceeding our way to the Victoria Falls Hotel."

Tom said, "that is an unusual coincidence As my family is going there too. What is your first name?"

"My name is Lynne, sir."

"It's my pleasure to meet you Lynne; my name is Tom."

"Hello Tom," Lynne says (with a smile)

"Hello, Lynne. That's my father over their" Tom said.

Lynne brushed her dark hair to one side. Also looked in a direction where Tom was pointing in. This cute little smile came over her gorgeous face that seemed to electrify happy thoughts inside Tom. Tom turned gently to look in the direction of his father. Lynne stepped close to Tom. Tom smelt her fragrance Tom's heart skipped a beat. "Where are your parents now?"

Lynne "there on the other side," she says. "You can just see them sitting down at the tables through that window." It was her mum sitting by herself at that time large She also had a long stemmed wine glass in hair her hand smiling. Drinking a glass of red wine. It seemed like she was talking to somebody, but Tom could not see from their as the window frame was obscuring his line of sight.

"You have lovely parents;"

Tom said. Lynne said, "Thank you. You have a kind father too. Those your sisters."

Tom said. "Yes one is on the way to the restaurant are you going that way,"

Lynn says, "one was going to walk down by the swimming pools and have a look around."

Tom butted backing nervously and said, "Well, I suppose we will catch up later if we don't see each other before then we'll meet at the Victoria Falls." What an excellent idea, the gorgeous Lynn said. "See you again soon Tom. :-)" A big smile from Tom and then Lynne walked sweetly on past Tom down the steps she went. Tom walked through the restaurant into the bathroom. Thinking to himself,

Tom was wondering if he will meet again. He rushed into the toilet. Used the bathroom, washed his hands. Came back out as quickly as possible. Walk through the restaurant area across the marble floors still looking through the window to see if he could see Lynne's mother but she was nowhere around to be seen. So Tom carried on walking back down the ramp to the steps, and a little path leading back to his father and sisters where they were waiting. Tom gazed around to see if he could see her in the pool area, but to no avail he could not see her. She seemed to have disappeared as if by magic. But Tom will never forget that magic moment on the stairs in the doorway. Is it an opportunity that was missed? Tom things to yourself and puts this down to a learning experience.

The children's father says, "let's get going let's go back to the vehicle and make our way to the Victoria Falls Hotel."

We all agreed on this and another road trip "I'm sure my father just loves driving."

("One, i.e., thinks we are all in agreement with that.") As he only seems to stop just for the rest. He was always on the go. The family prepared to leave and walked Up the winding path and the steps, we went. Past all the weaver birds and the blossoms on trees. I must say… A beautiful place where we were. We did not succeed to see everything there as there was so much more to see but what Denise and Amanda and Tom had seen will always be in their memories. Particularly for, Tom. Speaking to this gorgeous girl. Furthermore having a confidence to pass the time of day with her was just one of those wonderful experiences that will always be a memorable lesson of romance for Tom and the young beautiful girl Lynne.

Amanda shouts out "shotgun!" Again as soon as we managed to see the car in the car park.

Amanda she just like sitting on the front seat. Signifies used to make all sorts of excuses car sickness, etc. but still she is my sister, and the eldest girl suppose we must make way for the oldest in the family. Into the car, we pile into the car making sure everything is correct and safe.

Denise and I looked through the car window towards the hotel as we are driving off and then suddenly I seen Lynne getting into her mom's car with her father. As we drive past them, I gave her a wave. But I'm sure she did not see me. But I remember her. Keeping this little secret to myself to save any embarrassment, while the father is driving off and away from the hotel. We are Finally on the main road, and Amanda was reading the map. She was getting good at this.

We talked about the weaver birds and how cute that the little bird was sitting at our table, taking the paper rolled up napkins off us and wove them into his nest. Laughing if it was going to rain. However, that would not make any difference since it is not the rainy season yet. Aforementioned only passes the time as we have approximately one-hour drive to the Victoria Falls Hotel we are all excited to get there.

And to relax in what is supposed to be the best hotel yet. As cloudy mentioned earlier, but she explained how beautiful the star rated hotel was.

More potholes in the road dad had to slow down as it was getting quite dangerous to drive the speed. He has always been a more sensible driver. Driving down the lovely straight road, but still dodging potholes. Father Denise and Amanda was having a conversation, but. But Tom was not listening as he was deep in his thoughts of a young girl that he met about half an hour ago. "Hey," Dad, "look at this!" And he slowed down while a herd of wild animals with Longhorn's walked across the road. As he got closer, the animals just seemed to disappear into the thicket of the Bush. They were a golden colour with Longhorn and white bellies. Aforementioned was such a beautiful sight to see.

And then moments later we saw a lorry that had turned over and crashed on the side of the road. It had been totally stripped bare you could see this as we drove past very slowly because of the potholes in the road. And then suddenly about a half mile in the distance down the road. We saw a young boy inside a large lorry tyre; about six children having fun pushing rolling him down the street they looked like they were having such fun. The tire must have been from that large lorry that happens to be identified only a mile or two back.

Well, not too far now Amanda shouts out! We are nearly there. And sure enough there was the archway with assigned Victoria Falls Hotel the arch stood made out of 2 massive tusks that this monumental entrance must have obtained made out of concrete. As we drove underneath the welcoming sign of the archway, the gardens around just were a lovely lush green, and the sprinklers were working. The hotel was just a fabulous place to see. Again massive archways. It was a big building. We pulled up outside and parked up in front of the hotel doors. Right children we are here.

We did not require being addressed twice. As we each jumped out of the car. Dad said accompany me please, and the car will be okay there. We all walked into the reception lobby. Cloudier was right the five-star hotel was decorated Beautifully with highly polished marble floors. Oakwood beams and a set of excellent elephant tusks with a big brass gong hanging from brass chains. These are the most prominent real elephant tusks I have ever seen said our father. We all walked up to the check-in desk dad gave him his credentials were complete. In exquisite English, the concierge said, do you need any assistance with your luggage. Father agreed on this for the luggage to be taken up to the rooms. Would you like to have a beverage indoors bar area before y' all go to your rooms? Father agreed on this. And took the keys, and we all walked around to the bar area. Dad had a large African beer and we all have pineapple juice each. It was just exquisite the finest Hotel that we had ever have the pleasure of Everywhere continued air-conditioned the plants and Gardens were incredible. Just looking out of the bar by the large swimming pool. There were unusual plants hanging that look like orchids in all different colours. Deckchairs thatched parasols around the pool there was a small diving board at one end of the pool. Tom was so excited he could not wait to jump into the swimming pool. But we all know we had a few moments to wait before our rooms were right. After finishing and drinks the Porter came back and said your rooms already. Father said yes we were already also so let's go and have a look at chambers. We walked around the Portland area, and we could see what looks like a multi-storey building with Belconnen's looking out over the swimming pool. Into the core building, we went following the Porter. Up to the topmost floor, we went to the lift. The list went up as were all crammed into this lift with these the Porter stood there still as a rock while he was waiting while operating the lift. I noticed the buttons he pushed in a code, and he used a key. Then the door opened it looked like a lift and taken straight to the living room of a fancy suite. Porter showed us the left-hand side door the master bedroom suite on the right-hand side door is a single bedroom, and the next door is a double bedroom off the corridor. If you need anything, please Ring this Bell Andrew the Butler will serve you. He is also your personal chef if you so wish to dine in the penthouse apartment. Your keys sir. Oh yes, thank you, Father said to the Porter. There was a television in the apartment rooms and also a little bar area. It was an absolute excellent place to entertain. Most people that I know what would be quite jealous of a beautiful house like this I'm sure to this day that I would love a house like this. Then the Porter prepare to show us out onto the balcony, and we had a fantastic view over the swimming pools also we'all can observe spectacular mist of the Victoria Falls in the distance. The Porter explained that the Africans called the Victoria Falls the (Mussy-Atunyer) Loosely translated into English The smoke that thunders. Also, he pointed out in the distance of which we could see very clearly as it was not too far away in walking distance we had a great representation of the gorge itself. The Porter was wearing a long red jacket. Black sleeve also cuffs two gold stripes on the sleeves. He had loads of badges on the lapels. Looked very smart indeed with his red tie and red and black top hat and white shirt with a logo of the Victoria Falls Hotel on his left breast pocket of his jacket. The view from the balcony was astounding you can see the round archways all in white it looked like that we were in the palace. The Porter says this is the penthouse suite of the hotel the last person to stay here was their president just two days ago. President KK Kounder this is his favourite sweet. The porter then showed us back into the room, and so does the bathroom suite and a Jacuzzi. Then he strolled silently up to the door. As he got there, he said is there anything else you require Sir. To the father. Father said that would be all thank you. You have been very very helpful. Father handed him a tip. The gentleman walked out of the room into the lift, and the doors closed the two girls screaming and ran into their rooms. I went into my single room. Wow, this is fantastic I have an enormous double bed all to myself and my balcony. There was a small chair by the window, and two bedside tables with lamps on the ceiling were white with plaster moulding all the way around it there were speakers and the music center in the room. And a set of wardrobes built into the wall. I unlocked the closet, and all my clothes had been laid out for me on the hangers, and my socks were folded and placed on their shelves. We did not have to do a single thing to do with unpacking. Everything was picture perfect. Ran Around and jumped onto his bed, and Tom just sank into the bed linen. He sank into the soft, comfortable mattress. Although he was lying on his back looking up at the ceiling. Relaxing understanding was absorbing the atmosphere. The sun was beaming through the window. It was time to get changed into swimming costume, but, the place was that beautiful everywhere you looked was designed correctly in Tom's eyes. Tom could hear the girls saying look at this. Tom walked steadily out of his room, to the girl's room. Their room was all in white; they had a four poster bed in each room. The furnishings of each room were 2nd to none. But they did not have a balcony on that side. They just have a small glass terrace that felt like a hot greenhouse when you walked into it. That was just so exciting. The two girls said they felt like princesses. Father's room was the biggest room of all. The master bedroom is enormous! A large walk-in wardrobe a bathroom and a small living room area. We could live like this forever! But it's time to get ready and out we must go to the swimming pool. The girls already dressed in their swimming costumes. We all piled into the lift down to the ground floor furthermore walked out to the swimming pool Tom ran and jumped into the pool. The pool was to die for on the skin. It is just excellent. Everything was so worth it. The girls soon followed and before you know it we were all in the swimming pool including dad.

There was a lay-low a float in the swimming pool. Tom commandeered this immediately. A moment later Tom was lying down, relaxing floating on his back on the lay-low raft looking into the clear blue sky as the sun sets. While the girls were playing in the swimming pool making ripples in the pool. The water was rocking the lay-low gently. The sun was beginning to establish the horizon in a tropical paradise. A helicopter flew overhead what looked like a giant sunny logo painted on the side. It was pure bliss; Tom was thinking about oneself. While he was lying on the lay-low floating around in the pool. Then suddenly without any warning Tom was tipped into the pool as dad came up swimming underneath him like a killer whale swimming to attack. Bashing into the lay-low and tossing Tom into the air like a rag doll, landing into the water, he went. It's a fun family time; we all had a massive water fight. Everybody was fighting to get onto the lay-low including father. Was so much fun frolicking in the pool? We were in there for hours it was so beautiful and refreshing. There was a small area where you can swim up to get drinks at the bar was very close to the water edge. If you required a drink all, you had to do was ask. The waiters will bring you one. It was just stunning, idyllic fantastic, gorgeous I cannot entirely explain how excellent the Victoria Falls Hotel is it's so safe plus beautiful. All that you can think of they have there. And I mean everything. Whatever your wishes and desires are. Your heart could deliver requests at this romantic hotel.

Evening

Did not take the family long to get changed and proceeded to the main reception where all the entertainment was just starting. A classic disco lights and music all held in idyllic settings. With lots of interesting light for dancing on the dance floor and standing by the bar. A handful of people scattered around the table in the shadows of candle light. Dad found a table close enough to the dance floor so we could watch and enjoy the evening as it Unfolded. Tom looked around the place to see if he could see the gorgeous Young girl again. However, for all he saw he could not see her at all. A weak heart was feeling. As she did not appear while he looked. Amanda Denise and Tom were all sitting around a table with their father. Suddenly without any prompting dad jumped up with a big glowing smile on his face instantly started to dance some pretty fancy moves in front of the table making the children were and giggled. So happy feelings Entertaining, around the table. Dad was always good with things like that just breaking the ice and showing us some fancy moves with his dancing skills. It certainly worked as the girls jumped up and started dancing with dad. Then Dad stretched out his hand to Tom also. From this time forward we are all now the participants of nightlife culture succeeding to comprehend the nightclub education, it was too late to escape the magic of the dance. The whole family was entranced hypnotically dancing to their father's rhythm and the music. Dad turned around and started to dance towards the dance floor the children followed as if he was the Pied Piper of the discotheque. Father was very smooth on the dance floor. None of us felt embarrassed we were all just having fantastic fun. The natural Dancing King, our Father, was that night. Everyone undividedly took rolls dancing in the middle of the group circle of our family and the dancing friends. Showing our moves and new people started to join in. Everybody was smiling and enjoying the music and dancing to his or her hearts content. They can say our little family was within life and soul of the evening. The music played on to the early hours of the morning through the night we danced. Dance dance, wherever the may be because we are the Lords of the dance, says he. We all were dancing the dance and enjoyed every moment of it meeting new people making new friends. "this is what we do. Nightclubbing." Father said. Taught us a valuable lesson. The music played on, but their father left the dancefloor and bought some refreshments from the bar and place them on the family's table. Father sat down watching us enjoying ourselves on the dancefloor. Only minutes must have passed before we knew it there was a young lady chatting to daddy. She seemed very nice and had a lovely flirting smile. However, we did not take much notice as we all were having so much fun on the dancefloor with the new friends that we have met. Just looking occasionally to see father at the table still talking to the lady. Amanda leaned forward and told Denise that dad has just kissed that lady. Denise and Amanda looked astonished. Tom turned around the moment and could see the woman leaning over the table kissing their daddy. It was not a lengthy kiss; it was just a little bit longer than a greeting kiss. However, nevertheless dad had indeed met this delightful lady. Music changes tempo slowed smoochy songs came on. It was time to find a partner father was already on the dancefloor with the woman that he met before. She seemed quite nice and very attractive Amanda managed to find a young Italian boy; Denise stands in there alone for a moment. Their young boy came up and asked Denise to dance nervously Denise excepted. It was just Tom looking for somebody to dance with him. The record of the slow dance is halfway through when Tom finally seen someone that had been looking at Tom through the evening. So Tom approached the girl nervously. Asked her to dance? Here was the 1st slow dance that Tom had ever had. Not knowing what to expect. However, Nervously clumsily approaching the dance floor, holding the young girls hand gently. Tom can feel the soft touch of the girl's hand, in his hand. Nervously not knowing what to expect. The helpful smile from his dad Sent the according message for Tom to relax with this gorgeous young girl in his arms. As they both started to sway gently to the music, The evening was filled with new things that Tom was experiencing. 2 min later the slow record ends, and another slow record starts. Tom liked this song, so did the young girl that they were dancing together. A little nervous giggling from the girl in the conversation as they were both dancing. The young girl soon calmed down. Tom's calming inner voice soon relax the girl on the dancefloor. For This happened to be the 1st Slow dance ever with a girl as she had never done this before with a boy either. Seriously Something innocently romantically familiar with the two young people. What were these feelings that Tom could feel? As she also had never felt these feelings before. The soft voice of the young girl that Tom could hear played exciting feelings within his mind that he could not explain. The young girl, which Tom was dancing in a midst of Her aura. Was smiling, oh so sweetly. She seemed so sweet and gentle. It was smoothness that poetry was made for as their conversation bounced to each other, this young girl without knowing it is just sensing the 1st stages of romance. Likewise with Young Tom.

He could sense his heart beating in the rhythm of not only music, but of the girl that was in his arms.

Tom was sure she could be feeling the same way, both of them not knowing what these new feelings are. Only felt what is the natural hormonal drug that coursed through their veins. Bringing a smile on each other's faces and letting out natural pheromones between each other as they floated around in their world around the dance floor romantically together. Suddenly the room felt empty it seemed like they were the only people on the dancefloor looking into each other's eyes intensely. A few comforting words were spoken with each other as they danced. Romance is blooming.

Tom had nothing on his mind except for the incredible feelings that he was experiencing from this young girl in his arms. He pulled her closer and now identified the couple are perfect cheek to cheek as the music played on. The sweet scent of her hair enveloped Tom's nostrils as inhaled as much of this beautiful scent as he could. The music played on and on record after record as the DJ spun the vinyl as the evening drifts past the midnight hour and onto 3 AM in the morning. The young girl in his arms was distracted, as her mother called her. Tom had not even managed to get her name. As the young American girl thanks Tom for the dance, and walked off the dance floor looking over her shoulder while she slowly walked towards her mother standing at the edge of the dancefloor. The woman was waiting to hold her hand out for her daughters. As she approached. Also, then together they left. Tom stood for a moment and watched the little hint of romance walk out of the nightclub. Also out of his life for the time being or then he believed. The excitement of adrenaline just exploded in Tom's body encouraging a massive happy feeling in his mind body and spirit. The lights came on, and floodlit the dancefloor brilliant white light interrupted the evening, and the music stopped playing.

Tom walked steadily over to the table where his family was sitting enjoying their drinks. Father said that. It is time to go to the penthouse suite; this evening has come to an end. He can see we have all enjoyed the night. Tom's father said to the daughters. Everybody in the family loved that night. It unmistakably had a touch of romance to it. So their spirits were high and ultimately enjoyable. The family made their way out to the pool where it remained lit with underwater lights. The water in the swimming pool was standing calm and surreal. The gentle sound of crickets as they played their early morning melody. The birds were just starting to wake as they could hear the occasional chirp including a song as the sun was beginning to light up the distant horizon it would not be long until the new day arrived.

Step after step is walking past the swimming pool quietly listening to the conversations of other people talking amongst themselves as they walked to their rooms. It was not long before the children, and their father were safely in the penthouse suite. Father make sure that all the children were safely tucked up in bed before he managed to settle down himself.

Tom was lying on the bed looking at the drawn curtains in his room wrapped up in a comfortable feeling of a fantastic evening, as he drifted off to sleep. Entering the dream world of romance as the feelings of the night and the beautiful girl still enveloped his mind as he dreamt of the lovely evening with this beautiful girl that had entered into his senses. Still dancing in his dream the colours were so vivid as they both floated around the dance, this gave him time to think and rehearse within these romantic feelings. Suddenly he felt something pulling him away from the dancefloor also out of his dream he did not want to move or even leave his dream. Embattled emotions just to shut out this disturbing noise, as Stronger as he could ignore the voice from the dark while still holding onto the hope. There, it was again a small sound in the background. Tom'S name has pulled him out of his alpha sleep. The voice Had called this time, good morning Tom loudly. Tom was proceeding out of his dream as the bright colours of the dancefloor dissipated. The feelings of the girl in his Imagination of his arms faded with every sound, and movement the girl decreased. Then vanished into the darkness of the dream without a trace. Along with Tom's hope of completing this thought to what his heart desired. Tom was feeling a spatial awareness of his body sinking into the mattress. His earthly senses were coming alive. Then gradually Tom opened his eye to see a bright light from the window in the room shining from the window. It took moments for his eyes to customised to the dazzling sunshine.

We are all going for breakfast will thou like to join us.

Tom sleepily rubbed his eyes and looked again to see his father smiling so gently and so nicely also asking him once again would oneself like to come for breakfast.

Tom nodded sleepily. Not realising where he was for those few short moments as he came back into reality from his dream sleep. 9:30 AM in the morning and everybody had been up for at least 30 min. Tom hopped out of the comfortable bed as his dad left the room. Tom was Pulling on his dressing gown and walking out the boudoir and into the living room. To the breakfast area where everybody was sitting on the balcony then served by the Butler.

Denise pulled back the chair and patted the seat with her hand. Encouraging Tom to sit down next to her. Of which Tom obliged. Additionally, he said (sleepily) Thank you. The Butler was pouring Tom a large glass of fresh orange juice and offered him a menu of breakfast cereals laid out on the trolley. Tom pointed at of which he would like.

The Butler served Tom placed his cereal bowl on the table filled with his favourite cereal. The Butler left it up to Tom for him to pour his cold milk. Tom sprinkled a teaspoon of sugar onto his cereal after pouring the cold milk. In addition looking out over the fabulous scenery, the view was impressive. Perfect paradise.

Dad broke into the conversation and asked everybody if he or she enjoyed the evening. Thou are now nightclub veterans (he said. With a smile.) Denise says 'dad is the one Pied Piper of the dancefloor the king! Of-the-dance.' A Little giggle from the two girls and a happy feeling flowing around the breakfast table.

Amanda says it was that lady thou wish to see last night dad. Don't change the subject. By pointing out something of non-particular importance in the opposite direction to avoid answering complicated, tricky question. Amanda had learnt this lesson before in addition ignored the trickery of his placebo pointing in any non-specific direction. Amanda brings the conversation back into the room. However sister's asks the question again who was the lady; Dad was kissing. Father pulled back his hand and smiled (knowing there was no escape) and said you have seen me then. Caught red-handed Denise and Tom said together. Just a lady was enjoying a holiday here. For this was the last night, she implied that she was going back today to her hometown in Rhodesia.? With her daughter, Amanda stipulated. for whom which Tom was is dancing with. Tom blushed, as an embarrassing feeling flooded over him. Leaning forward grabbing his orange juice, drinking. Getting cover from the large glass as is the hot flush his rosy red, uncomfortable face flush. Burnt beacon across the table cunningly concealed or so he thought As the flush of embarrassment subsided. Tom placed his orange juice back on, the table. The look around the table as everybody had managed to dance and find an attractive partner that evening. So everybody was guilty. So did everybody have an enjoyable evening that night his or her father said. So everybody cracked under the strain of the embarrassing moment around the table, then the embarrassment as mentioned earlier entirely subsided as we were all together in the same boat. Denise said what about that young Italian boy was dancing with Amanda. Oh, he was so nice Amanda said. Am meeting him at the swimming pool today. That will be so sweet Denise says, am also meeting a friend by the swimming pool. Tom looked a little bit sad incident is serial knowing full well that his friend, whom he met that night was already on their way home to Rhodesia. Additionally, he would probably never see her again. However, am sure dad was a lot more experienced in this department. Additionally, we are all confident that he had taken some contact information from the lady that he was dancing with and seen kissing that night. Dad then pointed out the balcony to a few unusual man running across the road in the distance. In addition, disappearing.

Did oneself see that children? Now, what father what was it.? Oh, nothing it must be the gardeners or some workers finishing their shift. Children can seriously see the muscular Tonia missed floating up through the rainforest from here their dad says. It is a beautiful view. Again father managing to change the subject from the lovely lady, he was kissing that very evening. A pretty secretive person their father was in relation to girls.

The family was thinking nothing more of this as the five strange, suspicious uniformed men had disappeared off the footpath. Within the rainforest. Father had mentioned before that they looked like they were workers. So they were in uniform.

Father mention after breakfast that he had some business to take care of, plus he would be free after the afternoon Because this important meeting will only take a couple of hours. What is the meeting about Amanda said as she is the oldest? Father explained that there was a copper mine nearby needing new lines and belts for their machinery. So he was just giving them a quote for the installation from Mitchell Cotts. Of which he was the newly appointed partner director. The Butler approached the table, in addition, cleared away the empty bowls and plates. We all sat back enjoying the early morning sun on the balcony. Right, it has time for everybody to get dressed. What is it would like to do one think, about relaxing by the swimming pool, would be a lovely idea said Amanda? That will be superb,

Father said. Will set everything up so, thou have somebody to look after all while am having the meeting. The meeting is at 11 o'clock, and we should be back by 1:30 PM. Also, we can all have walked out to Victoria Falls. Just get a closer look of the largest curtain of water in the world. How would thou like those kids? Big smiles and yes we would love that father.) Right then let's get ready, and we can go down to the swimming pool. Also, enjoy the sun. Looking out over the balcony, we can see that Paul was getting quite full already with lots of friendly people. So the date is set, and this is what we will do. After the family had agreed on this, it did not take long for them all to get ready. Also, they were soon sitting down by the swimming pool relaxing on the sun loungers. Amanda's friend was nowhere around. Also, Amanda was looking quite sad. For she was missing that handsome young man that she had met that evening. That appeared not to take Tom long to plunge into the soothing pool. After father introduced us to a gray lady. That was going to look after us or keep an eye out for us while dad was at his business meeting. Her name was Margaret. She did not mind looking after us. As she was one of the staff at the hotel. A quick wave and kiss goodbye from the children's father and he soon disappeared off into the hotel. The children were free to experience the wonderful day as it unfolded. In the safety and comfort that they were being watched by Margaret.

Denise Amanda and Tom were watching the other children diving into the pool. So they were watching one young girl learning how to jump. Hands on the air knees together eyes closed bend the knees and jumps in headfirst breaking the water surface with their hands at the same time. Again and again she tried. Each time is getting a little bit better. So the girls and Tom decided to have a go at this and were soon making friends around the pool. Amanda did not seem to be too comfortable with diving in the swimming pool. However, Denise and Tom soon got the hang of this and were diving in like real professionals within a couple of hours. While Amanda took her time up by sunbathing and drinking long cocktails filled with fruit. As Amanda was 18 at the time. Margaret came over and offered us all some suntan lotion as we can see that we were getting quite red from the sunshine. Tom and Denise occasionally went to the swimming pool bar and relaxed in the water next to the swimming pool bar. With a long refreshing drinks and great company and friends around them that they met that day. It was so much fun enjoying the beautiful sunshine and their new friends that they had met. Suddenly everybody looked up in the air. As a large green helicopter flew over the hotel very low in the sky and disappeared over the treetops. The noise of the old engines was very loud making a thumping noise in the air as the helicopter went. Some of the parents around the pool called to their children in as they seemed quite nervous. However, innocently Denise Amanda and Tom did not take any real notice of this helicopter. Except just for looking at it innocently thinking that it was just a helicopter. The other parents were knowing full well that this was a military helicopter including the soldiers on board. Heading over towards the rainforest in that direction. The helicopter started Hovering Over the top of Victoria Falls. We could hear the aircraft in the distance, but y'all could not see it. Also, then the helicopter sound disappeared.

Printed in the United States
By Bookmasters